THEY CAME TO FORT YUMA

Luke Faraday—A bounty hunter who lived by his Hawken .50 rifle, he knew the territory would never be safe as long as the Bodine gang ran wild.

Lorene Martin—Most at home with the wild wind in her hair, behind her proper beauty she was a straight shooter protecting secret papers that could expose the vicious treachery of a California congressman.

Lieutenant Horatio Stack—Ashamed of letting his prisoner escape, he set out on the hard and lonely trail to bring Bodine in.

Chastity Blaine—A true daughter of the West, full of life—and now dangerously close to a cruel death at the hands of Bodine.

The Stagecoach Series
Ask your bookseller for the books you have missed

STAGECOACH STATION 8:
FORT YUMA

Hank Mitchum

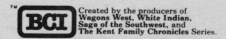

Created by the producers of
Wagons West, White Indian,
Saga of the Southwest, and
The Kent Family Chronicles Series.

Executive Producer: Lyle Kenyon Engel

BANTAM BOOKS
TORONTO · NEW YORK · LONDON · SYDNEY

STAGECOACH STATION 8: FORT YUMA
A Bantam Book / published by arrangement with Book Creations, Inc.
Bantam edition / October 1983

Produced by Book Creations, Inc.
Executive Producer: Lyle Kenyon Engel.

ISBN 0-553-23593-1

Published simultaneously in the United States and Canada

STAGECOACH STATION 8:

FORT YUMA

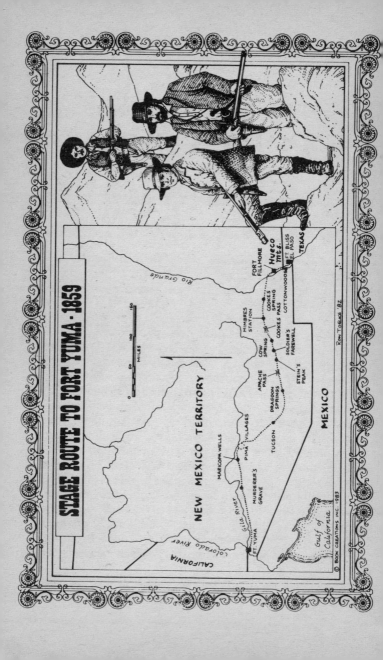

Chapter 1

Luke Faraday hitched his gun belt and sniffed the late-morning air. A breeze blew from the Rio Grande toward the American side, where El Paso sprawled in the sun. Grape pickers prowled the fields, and the sour smell of onions wafted across the river from the Mexican bank of the silt-laden river. The main street was crowded, just as Luke had expected. Departures of the Overland Mail Company stage were still an event nearly a year after John Butterfield started the ambitious undertaking, and the arrival of outlaw Ernie Bodine added to the festive atmosphere. The troops would be bringing him in from Fort Bliss at any moment. Faraday looked in the direction of the fort, three miles away, and drew in a breath. He didn't want to miss seeing Bodine's face one last time. But he saw no telltale dust trail and knew there was time before the troopers arrived. He patted the fringed bag on his hip, then adjusted the powder-horn thong that crisscrossed the strap holding the bag. His knife was well in the back so that the powder horn did not slap against the knife's elk-horn handle. His Colt .44 Navy revolver was loaded, all six cylinders, the hammer resting on a space between the cylinders.

He made his way toward the saloon next to the post office, directly across from the stage stop. His gray eyes

1

flickered over the crowd. Luke was taller than most, and men stepped aside as he passed. In his boots he stood well over six feet, and he walked on the balls of his feet like a prizefighter, his sidling gait deceptively graceful. A thick mustache bloomed under his aquiline nose. His lean facial features were accented by high cheekbones beside the thin bridge of his nose. A thick shock of dark hair flowed from under his Stetson to a point midway down his neck.

It would be cool in the Riverbank Saloon—a good place to have a taste of the fine El Paso wine to celebrate Ernie Bodine's return date with the hangman at Fort Yuma.

"Hey, Faraday," yelled a man standing next to the stagecoach. "You want to ride shotgun to Yuma with me?"

The stage driver, Morty Tubbs, stepped away from the Concord, fluffing out his full beard with a gnarled hand. He hobbled toward Faraday on bandy legs, his worn bootheels making him totter from side to side. He spat a stream of brown tobacco juice into the dust of the street and stuck out an arm to bar Luke's way.

The tall man with the smoke-gray eyes stopped in his tracks and looked down at the man built like a barrel keg. He grinned, exposing even, white teeth. "Hey, old hoss," Luke said. "I'm on my way to spend some hard-earned money on a glass of wine. I'll buy you some dust solvent if you'll walk in with me."

"I know, I know, Luke, and you got a right to a taste, catching Bodine and all, but there's a lady up there on the porch dyin' to meet you. Young filly, just in this morning from St. Louie, and all she jabbers about is you and Bodine."

Luke's eyes shifted toward the shaded porch of the stage-line office. A cluster of men and women in traveling garb stood underneath the hanging sign that read Butterfield Stage Stop—El Paso. The dim outline of the word Franklin was still visible on the sign. The name had been changed a few months earlier. Benjamin Franklin Coontz had named the settlement after himself when he was appointed the first postmaster in 1852. Now the town had a

Spanish name, in deference to the neighbors across the border.

Luke scanned the valises and handbags that were stacked on the porch. The people looked as weary as their dusty luggage. "They in from St. Louis? News of Bodine hasn't hardly had time to get that far yet."

"Word of his recapture was at Fort Chadbourne from the eastbound," Tubbs explained. Then he pointed toward the porch of the station. "There she is. You stay right where you are, Luke. I'll fetch her. Mail ain't ready yet, and I got to wait for Bodine. So we got time for introducin'."

Luke said nothing. He stood there, his weight heavy on one foot, looking up and down the street. There were more people in town than he'd ever seen at one time. Bodine was big news in the settlement.

The Concord coach creaked in the sun as one of the lead team took up slack in the traces. Another horse flicked its tail at a clutch of flies. A young man threw a carpetbag onto the roof, where the man above jammed it in among the rest of the luggage. The stage was due to have left at eleven o'clock, as it always did on Saturday. It was drawing near the quarter hour, Luke figured, and still no sign of the troopers and Bodine.

Morty hobbled up the steps and disappeared in the huddle of passengers. A moment later he reappeared, holding the wrist of a young woman. She steadied her straw hat with one hand as Tubbs led her down the steps and across the street to where Faraday stood waiting.

"This here's Miss Chastity Blaine," Tubbs announced, thrusting the girl toward Luke.

"Pleased to meet you," Luke said.

"Are you Mr. Faraday, the bounty hunter?"

"I'm Luke Faraday."

"But you brought in that killer—Bodine."

"I did."

"I'm mighty grateful, Mr. Faraday. My father was assistant warden when Bodine escaped and killed the warden."

Luke looked at the girl closely. She was pretty. Her blue eyes sparkled like a mountain lake, and she seemed to have a peppery spirit. Upturned nose, heart-shaped face, she looked to be no older than nineteen, probably younger. Her blond hair dangled in ringlets down her cheeks, with the sunlight giving it a high sheen.

"Your pa's Vernon Blaine? He's acting warden now. He'll see to Bodine's hanging."

"Yes," she said, tight-lipped. "I would like you to be there."

Now Luke understood. Morty was using the girl to persuade him to ride shotgun. Well, maybe it would work out. There was nothing to keep him in El Paso. He could ride to Yuma with pay, and maybe all the way to San Francisco.

"I got to have a shotgun rider, Luke," Morty said lamely.

"Get a boy to fetch my horse and rifle, and I'll ride along," Luke replied, tipping his hat to the young lady. "I guess I could watch Bodine hang. No man deserves it more."

Chastity saw his gray eyes flicker, and she felt a chillness ripple up her arm. But she forced a smile. "I know my pa'll be grateful. He was mighty upset when the warden got murdered. I came all the way from back east to be with Pa."

"Yuma's no place for a young lady," Luke said disapprovingly. "But suit yourself."

He walked toward the saloon, more determined than ever to have that glass of wine. It might be the last for a while; it was a long, grueling trip to Yuma overland on the stage.

"I'll get the boy to tie your horse to the stage," Morty said gleefully, ushering the girl back to the porch. "And I'll have that drink with you, son!"

Luke did not look back. He was not a man who felt comfortable with innocent young women from the East. In his opinion, Chastity Blaine was walking into a situation she didn't understand. Her father was a blunderer and might even have been responsible, unwittingly or not, for Bodine's having escaped from Fort Yuma in the first place. A good man had died. And Bodine had cheated the hangman—for a time.

But beyond that, Yuma was a hellhole. It wasn't even a fort anymore, although people still called it that. It had been established in 1850 on the eastern side of the Colorado River, about half a mile below the mouth of the Gila River. The next year, it was moved to a low hill on the west bank, in an old mission. It was abandoned, then reactivated by the army in 1852, then abandoned again the following year. Now it was a prison, with cells that baked a man alive in the summer and froze him at night in the winter. Otherwise, Yuma was little more than a supply depot, which attracted every kind of criminal since it was the best southern emigrant route now that the Yuma Indians had been brought under control.

Yuma still existed largely because the stage route had been established through it two years ago, in 1857. And even that was still a matter of raging controversy. The wrangling over various proposed transcontinental stage routes for a mail-and-passenger stage line had come to a shuddering halt when by an act of Congress the thirty-second parallel route was established in March 1857, and John Butterfield and his associates were granted the contract. But even now, a year after service began in September 1858, there were many who were still howling about Butterfield and the choice of stage routes.

Luke never made it to the saloon.

As he stepped onto the boardwalk, a commotion up the street brought him to a halt. Heads turned and talk rose up like the sounds of magpies in a fruit-tree patch. Luke saw them coming, then—the troopers flanking their prisoner. A U.S. marshal led the procession.

Ernie Bodine sat defiantly in the saddle, his wrists manacled. A cold-eyed man in his late thirties, he had unusually small, pale-blue eyes set in a ferretlike face, which was grizzled from a three-day beard growing over the pocks that were residues from childhood. He had shaved off his beard only to alter his appearance, but Luke recognized him anyway, having tracked him for two months, never more than a day or two behind him until the last, when he had closed to within hours.

Luke had caught Bodine in the Hueco Mountains east of El Paso and had brought him in to Fort Bliss to claim the reward. He remembered the look on Bodine's face when he was cornered, out of food, low on ammunition, standing there on bowed legs, his knotted muscles working despite the fact that he knew it was all over. Luke had seen a badger in a trap once, gnawing off its leg, rabid from a skunk bite. Snarling and growling, the badger had lunged at him until it broke out of the trap and had to be shot through the head.

Bodine passed close, glaring at him. Luke smiled thinly, then nodded at the lieutenant.

Lieutenant Horatio Stack gripped the bridle on Bodine's horse and waved a gloved hand at the surging crowd, warning them away. He sat straight in the saddle, at attention as if on parade—spit and polish, immaculate uniform, regulation all the way from the tassels on his hat to the socks in his shiny boots. Stack was twenty-six years old, with close-cropped brown hair, blue eyes, a cleft chin, full lips that were almost feminine, and a large nose that jutted over smooth-shaven skin.

"Close in," Stack ordered the troops. "Keep that crowd back."

The passengers on the porch stepped forward, gawking at the manacled man surrounded by a lieutenant and four enlisted men in cavalry uniforms.

"Who is that?" asked a woman standing on tiptoe.

"A better man than those bluecoats herdin' him," answered a lanky cowhand leaning against the wall behind the crowd on the porch.

Chastity whirled on him, her face crimson. "Don't you know who that outlaw is?" she snapped. "He murdered the warden at Yuma Prison and escaped."

"We know who he is, lady," drawled the cowhand,

"but he ain't no outlaw. All he done was take an advance on his army pay!"

His companions guffawed, and Chastity, infuriated, clenched her fists and turned back to stare at the man who was the center of attention. The detail came to a halt a few yards behind the stage as Stack released his hold on Bodine's bridle and held up a hand. The marshal, Pete Brookins, grabbed the reins from the other side and held on.

A couple standing a few feet away from Chastity leaned their heads close together, exchanging whispered comments. Anne Jenkins, a pinch-faced woman with light hair and dark beads of eyes, could not hold down her whispers.

"I don't like it, Merle," she told her husband. "A convict riding on the stage with us!"

He glared at her and muttered something else in her ear. Jenkins then glanced at a tall man a few feet away and shook his head slightly as if to tell him he would see that his wife made no further outbursts.

The man, Congressman Hiram Cornwallis, snorted disdainfully as he fingered a clove from his vest pocket, slipping it into his mouth. Those around him could smell the whiskey on his breath, nonetheless. Next to him, his youthful aide, Stuart Gorman, looked at Chastity with undisguised admiration. But she did not take her eyes off the prisoner, and Stu wished he could command such rapt attention.

Morty Tubbs yelled at the luggage handlers to speed things up. He pulled a large watch from his pocket and eyed the time. "Where's that danged mail?" he hollered, stuffing the watch back in his pocket. No one paid him the slightest attention.

A boy tied a sorrel gelding to the rear of the coach. He carried a bedroll and a Hawken .50-caliber rifle in a fringed buckskin case. Another boy staggered under the weight of a California saddle. The baggage handler recognized the items and motioned for the boys to hand them topside.

Stack backed his troops up, then turned to the U.S. marshal flanking Bodine. "What's the delay here?"

"Mail, I 'spect."

"See if you can hurry it up."

The marshal released the reins of Bodine's mount and tapped spurs to his horse's flanks, sidling him up to Morty. "You best go get the mail yourself, Tubbs. The lieutenant's gettin' edgy."

"Hellfire. I got to do every danged thing around here!"

"Chastity . . . Chastity, where are you?"

Chastity turned and saw a woman pushing through a small throng of Mexican *peones,* nearly stumbling over a naked toddler as she hurried toward the stage station.

"Over here!" yelled Chastity.

Lorene Martin, wearing a long skirt beneath a new traveling coat with a high collar and carrying a carpetbag brimming with hastily purchased souvenirs, struggled to keep her straw skimmer on her flame-red hair—hair that seemed to be spun from burnished copper and brushed gold. She was tall, green-eyed, and obviously uncomfortable in such fancy clothes. She tripped coming up onto the porch, blew a strand of hair away from her mouth, and panted as she lurched to a stop next to Chastity.

"Thank goodness. I thought I had missed the stage," she said breathlessly. Her voice was low and husky. Her green eyes flashed as she saw the troopers and their prisoner.

"There seems to be a delay," Chastity explained.

"Is that the man?"

"Yes. That's Bodine."

"He—he seems quite fierce and desperate."

"I hate him," Chastity said impulsively.

Lorene drew a deep breath and patted her side, as if that would remove the stitch of pain there. Daughter of Randolph Martin, the retired chief of police of San Francisco, she was returning home from Washington, D.C., where she had picked up some documents for her father. Martin was in private practice now, and he had told Lorene only that the papers she would be carrying were of the utmost importance in a case he was working on—and utterly secret.

She frowned at Congressman Cornwallis, who was staring at her with what approximated a leer. She had met him in Washington and was surprised that he was to be her traveling companion all the way to San Francisco. The rumors she had heard about him made her wary of striking up any but the most superficial friendship with him. Yet he had been polite throughout the journey thus far, despite making a big show of drinking too much in the coach.

Lorene knew how Chastity felt about Bodine, but she also surmised that Chastity was fascinated with the man. She had talked of little else on the journey from St. Louis, explaining how Bodine and his partner, Chet Morgan, had been arrested for robbing an army payroll shipment and had been sent to Yuma Prison. All of the soldiers guarding that payroll, which came in from San Francisco, had been murdered by Bodine and Morgan, who were army privates. Both men were scheduled to be hanged on Friday, the seventh of October, and this was October first. Bodine, however, had escaped, killing the warden.

Word had reached the passengers in Fort Chadbourne that a bounty hunter had recaptured Bodine, who now was certain to keep his date with the hangman. Chastity kept praying for the stage to be on time so that she could see the man hang for his crimes. Lorene thought it was morbid of her to want to see such a thing, but detected a bit of pride that Chastity's father was now in charge of the prison and wanted her to join him there.

Lorene scanned the crowd of onlookers. Bodine seemed to be the center of attention, yet strangely aloof from the gawkers. Instead, he looked steadily in one direction. Lorene followed his look and saw the tall man in front of the saloon, towering above the other people around him: women in sunbonnets, men in battered wide-brimmed hats. This man was broad shouldered, wore a flat-crowned hat, chambray shirt, and thin leather vest, and he carried a Colt pistol in a holster. Slung across his massive chest were a powder horn and the strap to his buckskin bag. He wore the new trousers made by Levi Strauss that were made of material from some French town—Nîmes, she thought, so that it was called *de Nîmes,* or simply denims. His hat shaded his features, but she had the impression of a strong jawline and a mustache.

"Who is that?" she whispered to Chastity, nodding in Luke's direction.

"That's the bounty hunter who captured Bodine. Faraday. I met him."

"Is he going with us?"

"I—I think so. He said he would ride shotgun."

"Ummm," Lorene said, and Chastity gave her a sharp look. Lorene was in her twenties—not much older than Chastity, but far more mature, Chastity realized. She could ride and shoot, she was more at home on a horse than at the Washington teas she had spoken about, and she was homesick for her father's ranch in the Sonoma Valley, north of San Francisco.

Inside the post office, Morty checked the mailbags handed him by the postmaster. A stick was tied to the bags, branded with the legend: *San Francisco, California, Per Overland Mail. St. Louis, Sept. 19, 1859. Return Label by Express.*

"'Bout time," Morty spat. "We got passengers, Caleb."

"Had to wait for Missus Witherspoon's catalog order, Morty. Keep your pants on," the postmaster chided.

The bags were small, tied together so that if anything happened to the stage, the mail could be thrown across a horse and proceed to its destination. Each station added to the packets, and no stage could leave without the mail.

Morty hefted the bags, slung them over his shoulder, and stepped outside the post office.

"All aboard!" he called, turning to head for the empty stage. "Lieutenant, you can load your prisoner."

Stack nodded at Tubbs and then called out, "Troopers—dismount!" He opened his mouth to say something to Bodine, but his words were drowned out by a sudden burst of explosions.

Gunfire erupted from all directions. Women screamed,

and men dove for the ground. Stack's horse reared, and he fought the animal back down.

The crowd scattered like a flock of chickens. From the shadowed alleyways between buildings, white smoke belched from pistol and rifle barrels. Morty Tubbs backed toward the post office, confused. The horses hitched to the stage spooked and began kicking each other.

Two troopers reeled in their saddles as the first volley of shots caught them. One of them twitched, turned rigid, and tumbled back over the cantle. The other slumped over, half his face shot away. His horse twisted in a tight circle, the trooper's dead hands still gripping the reins.

Lieutenant Stack was jolted as another trooper's horse rammed into his. "Ambush!" he yelled, over the roar of rifles and pistols. Quickly, he leaped from his horse and scrambled under its neck. He reached for Bodine, trying to yank him from the saddle.

Bodine looked down and drew his booted leg up high. He kicked hard, the heel catching Stack in the chest. Stack staggered and fell as his legs went out from under him. He hit the ground sharply, his spine jolted from the impact. Through a haze he saw Bodine holding manacled hands to his reins, kicking his horse in the flanks.

Lieutenant Stack drew his pistol and cocked it. He raised his arm and tried to draw a bead on Bodine. Out of the corner of his eye he saw one of the ambushers riding a horse straight for him, smoke curling up from the man's big Colt Dragoon pistol. Stack stood up and leaped out of the way just as another pistol boomed. The ambusher twisted in the saddle as if struck in the side with a maul.

Stack saw Luke Faraday, in a crouch, already thumbing his hammer back for the next shot. Just then the ambusher's horse crashed into Bodine's. The rider, blood gushing from a lung wound, was hurled from the saddle to the dirt. The horse kicked up dust and scrambled away, with the other riderless mounts stampeding in its wake.

Stack aimed again at Bodine, but the escaped convict dove off the other side of the saddle. Suddenly another ambusher appeared on horseback. He leaped to the ground and, together with Bodine, jerked the wounded outlaw to his feet.

"Get me a horse!" croaked Bodine as their mounts bolted down the street after the other horses.

"Ain't any!" the other outlaw shouted.

Bodine cursed his manacles. He looked wildly around for a horse. "Over there!" he shouted to his companion. "The stage!"

The two remaining troopers yanked at their reins, trying to see through the smoke and dust. Brookins, the marshal, rode up, trying to sort out the enemy. A bullet knocked him out of the saddle, and he fell on top of Stack. Another trooper jerked as a bullet caught him in the back. He stiffened, fired his pistol with a reflexive squeeze of his finger, and slid headfirst to the ground, his eyes glazed with impending death.

Bodine and his companion dragged the wounded outlaw and shoved him through the door of the empty stage. Then they scrambled to the driver's box.

"Get 'em outa here, Rafe!" yelled Bodine.

The outlaw, Rafe Adams, jerked the bullwhip up from the floor and unwrapped the reins from around the brake. He released the brake and cracked the whip over the string of four horses, and the stage lurched into motion.

The last trooper started to give chase. Five outlaws appeared from between buildings now, converging on the stage. Two pistols boomed, and the trooper threw up both hands as lead thwacked into his flesh. His pistol flew into the air, did a slow loop, and clattered to the ground. The trooper stayed in the saddle for a few more seconds; then his horse ran out from under him, and he fell to the dirt.

Luke Faraday targeted one of the outlaws in his sights and squeezed the trigger. His Colt .44 bucked in his hand, and white smoke and orange flame belched from the barrel. The outlaw tumbled over, his body smacking into the horse's rump. His foot caught in the stirrup and he was dragged along, bouncing in the dust of the street. Luke took aim as the horses shot past him into the cloud of dust raised by the stage. He fired, and the last man in the bunch stood up in the stirrups and did a somersault over the horse's tail. He landed with a crunch, a gaping hole the size of a fist in his chest.

The stage, with Luke's horse tied behind, clattered away, raising a whorl of dust that engulfed the three remaining horsemen. The outlaw caught in the stirrup slipped free and rolled over three times before his body stopped dead, falling dust covering him with a thin patina of grime. He stared at the sky with vacant eyes that no longer saw anything at all.

As soon as the battle had ended, Lieutenant Stack had seen to loading a wagon with the dead and wounded troopers and had sent it ahead on the three-mile trip to Fort Bliss with a hastily written account of Bodine's escape. Now, after rounding up one of the army horses that had run away during the battle, he got ready to take after the outlaws.

"That wagon oughta be at Bliss by now," Morty Tubbs said as he came up beside the lieutenant. "Reckon they got troopers already on Bodine's trail. Won't take 'em long to catch up to that rascal."

"What about the marshal and that bystander?" Stack asked.

"Marshal's dead," the stage driver replied. "The civilian won't live out the hour."

"With the stage gone, does that leave you stuck here?"

"The mail's got to get through—it's John Butterfield's personal guarantee. We've got a big Concord in the barn. Don't use 'em much out here, but this one's used personal by Mr. Butterfield when he checks the line. A wheel broke down last time he rode through, and he left it behind for repairs. It's been patched up real good, but Mr. Butterfield sent word he'd be shipping a whole new wheel. Hell, it might squeak too much for a company president, but it oughta do for the likes of me. Team's a problem, though. Only horses we got left is the string we come into El Paso with, and they're plumb tuckered."

"You do what you have to do, Tubbs. Troopers from Fort Bliss should already have quite a head start on me, but I'll catch up."

"You goin' after Bodine?"

Stack tightened the last cinch on his saddle, then mounted his horse in a single, smooth motion.

"Bodine's my responsibility. I want to be sure he gets to Yuma. He deserves to hang double after what he did here."

Stack saluted Morty and spurred his horse. As the townspeople watched his horse step out, a buzz of conversation arose.

Luke Faraday watched him go, then walked over to where the stage driver was standing. "You'd better bring that other stage out if we're going to get started today."

"You still planning to ride shotgun?" Morty asked.

Faraday touched a hand to his holstered pistol. "My horse just left without me and I want him back."

"What about Bodine? You aim to mix with him again?"

"He's going to find a hard world out there."

Chapter 2

Rafe Adams drove the stage hard. Spools of dust twirled into the sky, leaving a telltale track behind them. The outriders rode well to the side, their own horses adding to the dust cloud in their wake.

Ernie Bodine kept looking back.

"See any sign of a posse?" Rafe asked.

"Nope. But that don't mean there won't be one."

"Reckon so," Rafe replied, his lips caked with trail dust and cracked from the sun. He and his men had waited for the right moment to free Bodine, but the cost had been high. He knew why, too. The troopers had been as dumb as they expected. It was that damned bounty hunter—Luke Faraday—who had put a kink in the rope. If he came after them, they'd have to do some quick thinking. Faraday was a tracker—one who kept on coming. A damned bloodhound. Well, during the escape he'd been shielded by the stage, nowhere near Bodine and the troopers, so they hadn't been able to hit him. The next time would be different.

Rafe Adams was a lean, taciturn man in his early forties. The years had turned him bitter, and the events of recent months had hardened that bitterness into a dangerous melancholy. He had been the mastermind behind the army payroll robbery that sent Bodine and his partner, Chet Morgan, to prison. They had all known each other

15

and had fought together in campaigns before the army split them up, sending Adams up to San Francisco, Bodine and Morgan to Fort Yuma. They had kept in touch through the mail and, fed up with low pay, had agreed to take the payroll and find new lives in Mexico.

Rafe was the outside man who engineered Bodine's escape from Yuma Prison—an escape that failed to free Chet Morgan, who was in solitary confinement at the time. And Rafe had just freed Bodine again. But there was no great love between the men—it was a simple matter of economics. Rafe wanted his share of the payroll loot, and he had no idea where it was. After the robbery, Bodine and Morgan had split the money, each stashing his half in a separate cache without telling the other its location. Now it was crucial to keep Bodine out of prison. Only then could Rafe be certain he would get his share.

Rafe was a wanted man himself, and it cost money to stay on the dodge. He was an army deserter, and he'd had the eerie experience of seeing a drawing of his face on posters from San Francisco to El Paso, complete with a notice of a four-hundred-dollar reward. He knew men who would kill for a quarter of that.

In the months following the arrest of Morgan and Bodine, Rafe had done a lot of serious thinking. It had been a hardscrabble life without his share of the payroll money, and there had been times when he would have liked to knot the rope to hang either or both men. He was rankled that they had hidden the loot and not told him where it was stashed. The robbery had been his idea, and he felt cheated. Now he no longer cared about sharing, equally or otherwise. Not with Bodine or Morgan. Perhaps not with anyone.

Instead, he had other plans. The minute Bodine recovered his half of the hidden money, Rafe planned to send him to hell, where he belonged. The men he had hired to spring Bodine in El Paso were handpicked—greedy men who would do his bidding as long as he dangled the promise of riches in front of them. But they, too, were expendable.

Bob Johncock was inside the coach. Every so often, they could hear his groans of pain. Riding on horseback alongside were Will Peeker, Jim Culhane, and Dan Rawlings. All were killers, good with knife, rifle, and pistol—or bare hands. They wouldn't like the dangerous task of springing Chet Morgan from prison, and neither did Rafe Adams. That was Bodine's plan. Rafe would just as soon have Bodine's full share and let Morgan rot. But he would have to watch his step with Bodine. Even with a gun at his head, Bodine would never tell where the money was hidden. He was that tough.

"Horses won't be able to keep up this pace," Rafe yelled over the noise of the team and the rumble of the coach.

Bodine wiped flecks of foam from his face, blown back from the near horse's mouth. He knew the animals were in danger of foundering. "Pull 'em up. We'll cut loose one of the stage horses for you to ride, and I'll throw a saddle on that one of Faraday's back there."

Rafe slowed the team, watching the road ahead. Spindly ocotillo cactus dotted the land, a broken land gouged with gullies and ravines. Yet the land in the Rio Grande valley was lush, teeming with life. The river flanked the road, and wild birds flapped up as they passed. Doves whistled by, and ducks banked and braked for a landing on the flowing waters. Here the road was better, much improved over the wild stretch out of El Paso. It would be that way, Rafe knew, clear to Cottonwoods Station.

There was a wide spot in the road—an old cattle trail leading to the river. Rafe turned the team onto it and hauled up on the reins. Bodine jumped down, and the three riders pulled in beside them.

"Cut those horses loose from the traces," Bodine ordered. "Couple of saddles up on top—get one on the best team horse, and I'll ride that gelding hitched to the boot. We'll bring the others as spares."

Rafe swung down, holding his temper in check. Bodine didn't even know these outlaws Rafe had recruited, and already he was taking charge.

Will Peeker, slouching in the saddle, gave Rafe a questioning look. Rafe nodded, his lips set tightly together. Jim Culhane and Dan Rawlings started scrambling onto the coach. Dan tossed Faraday's saddle down to Peeker, who stood waiting for it. Meanwhile, Culhane started throwing baggage off the top, looking for another saddle. Soon the ground was strewn with suitcases, carpetbags, boxes, and crates.

"Ain't no other saddle," said Culhane, a dark-haired man with bushy eyebrows and a pencil-thin mustache. His hands touched a pair of long crates, but he decided to leave them alone. They were marked Dry Goods—Awnings.

"Well, Rafe," Bodine smirked, "looks like you gotta ride bareback to the next stop."

Rafe unhitched the stage horses, all the while concealing the burning anger in his gut. Quickly, he shortened the reins on his mount, tied the horses to the stage, then went to the rear of the coach to see what Bodine was up to.

"See what they got in the boot," Bodine ordered.

Rafe stood by, looking over the trail behind them. He was nervous. Troopers or a posse could come at any time. Two of the others—pudgy Will Peeker and lanky Dan Rawlings—were going through the bags with Bodine, who though handicapped with the manacles, still managed to pocket a few coins and a silver belt buckle.

"What about Johncock?" Rafe asked.

"See if he can ride," muttered Bodine.

Rafe opened the door of the coach and looked inside. Bob Johncock was on the floor, chalk faced and in pain. Blood smeared the flooring where he had writhed in agony. Rafe felt a surge of queasiness roil his stomach.

"Johncock?"

"Damn, Rafe, I can feel the ball in me. You gotta get it out."

"Can you ride? We're mighty pressed for time."

"Hell, I could ride if you get me on a horse. But I got to get that ball out. Feels big as a watermelon."

Johncock was twenty-one years old. He had taken to the trail a couple of years ago after killing a man in St.

Louis. It was self-defense, but the man he killed was the sheriff's brother-in-law.

Rafe's jaw twitched, and he realized that he was grinding his teeth in anger. There was a hole in Johncock's chest, and a pink froth bubbled over his shirt. Likely the bullet had struck a bone—no telling what it had done after that.

"Turn over, Bob. I'll see if the ball came out."

"Oh, Jesus," moaned Johncock as he rolled over on his side. Rafe crawled partway inside the coach. There was no sign of an exit wound.

"Ball's still in there. Won't be easy to find."

Johncock gasped, choking on blood, and his dark eyes took on a faraway look—a look of fear. He rolled over on his back again and doubled up in pain.

"Hey, look at this, Rafe!" Bodine shouted.

"Be back in a minute, son," Adams said to Johncock. "You just hang on a little while."

"Will you lookee here!" exclaimed Bodine, holding up a woman's handbag and a pile of letters. "We done got us the ticket to bust old Chet outa Yuma! Then there'll be twice the money to go around!"

"What the hell, Ernie . . . Bob's—"

"In a minute. One of those passengers back there is Vern Blaine's little girl—name of Chastity Blaine. Chastity. How about that? Chas-ti-ty! Whooee, boys, we done got us some pay dirt here!"

"Dammit, Ernie, what's on your mind?"

Bodine grinned wide and shook the letters in Rafe's face, cackling with glee.

"Don't you see, Rafe? Blaine's little girl's going to Yuma to see her sweet old daddy. All we got to do is take her off the next stage, carry her up to the prison, and Vern's got to open them gates and let Chet out. Otherwise, he gets his daughter served up like wolf meat. There's even a picture of her."

Bodine shoved a yellowing tintype of Chastity Blaine into Rafe's face. He looked at the picture of the pretty blonde and realized he had seen her back in El Paso—first on the porch and later talking to Luke Faraday. Bodine was crazy, but it might work. Vernon Blaine was a widower, and his daughter was his only kin.

"Where you plan to get this gal?" asked Peeker, taking the picture from Adams. "She might turn back, you bein' loose and all."

"Cookes Pass," Bodine answered without hesitation.

"Good place," admitted Adams.

Peeker handed the tintype to Rawlings and sauntered back to the stage. "Johncock? We got you a horse. Can you ride?"

"I got to ride, Bill, else I'm done for."

"You'll make it, Bob."

Johncock was sitting up, determined to get out of the coach.

"You sit tight," Peeker said. "I'll get some help." He walked back to Bodine. "Johncock says he can ride."

"Well, let's pull outa here," Adams told Bodine. We've been here too long as it is. I'll give Peeker a hand with Johncock."

Bodine's face darkened, but he said nothing. Instead, he followed the men back to the coach. Peeker stood to one side as Rafe leaned over and reached for the wounded outlaw.

Bodine thrust both manacled hands forward and jerked Rafe's pistol from its holster. He cocked it as Rafe and Peeker froze, dumbfounded.

"What you aimin' to do?" asked Johncock as he saw Bodine with the pistol.

"Say good-bye, kid. We can't pack you."

Bodine fired point-blank. The pistol spewed white smoke and flame. Johncock's head jerked as the .44 ball smacked into his forehead just above his left eyebrow. He kicked a leg straight out, twisted to one side, and fell back. His boot twitched twice and lay still. The heavy stench of exploded black powder filled the coach.

Peeker muttered a curse under his breath, while Rafe licked his lips but said nothing. Rawlings came running up, saw what had happened, and retched, fighting down the bile that rose up in his throat. Jim Culhane had just finished saddling Faraday's horse for Bodine, tightening the cinch. Now he stood off by himself, his eyes narrowed to slits.

"I'll keep the pistol, Rafe," Bodine announced. "You got a spare revolver hanging from your saddle, Peeker."

"I reckon," said Peeker.

"Give it to Rafe."

Then Bodine rammed Rafe's pistol behind his waistband and strode back to the gelding. He grabbed the saddle horn with both hands and pulled himself up. "Let's ride," he said curtly.

Peeker started to say something, but clamped his lips tight. This was not the time. Bodine had drawn blood, and he had done it as coldly as Peeker had ever seen it done. It had been a question whether Johncock could have made it on horseback. But a man ought to stick by his friends. . . . And Bob Johncock had been a friend.

Cottonwoods Station lay twenty-one miles northwest of El Paso. The stage run took about five hours on good days. Bodine knew the route well, but he also knew that he had no more than an hour or two head start on any posse or army detachment. The army was the bigger worry—soldiers got paid, while possemen generally did not.

Rafe's stage horse had taken the hard ride well and had gotten its second wind. Riding without a saddle helped. Faraday's sorrel had good lungs and showed no sign of lagging. The others had changed mounts, and the stage horses seemed to be holding up. And Bodine pushed them all hard. It was important to get to Cottonwoods before the army or a posse could catch up. By pacing the horses, they ate up the miles until the cottonwood trees clustered on the horizon, a little before four that afternoon.

"There it is," said Rafe. "Want to scout it out?"

"Just ride on in. I've been through here—the stationmaster's alone. He won't know any better."

Orville Willits didn't know any better, until he saw Bodine's face—and Rafe Adams riding alongside. He had a new poster of Adams inside the adobe. The reward had been raised to five hundred dollars.

"Don't you move!" Bodine rammed the sorrel right up behind the man, hemming Willits in among the horses. He was unarmed.

Rafe hefted Peeker's big Dragoon pistol with both hands and held it on the stationmaster. "Just stand steady," he said.

Willits nodded numbly. He lived alone at the station. He had a deep well out back, and the Mexicans from nearby Mesilla brought him fresh vegetables. He hunted for his meat, but he had never shot a man—had never even thought about it. He was a prospector who had hit so many dry holes that he'd gotten smart and gotten out of the business. But the loner instinct still was strong in him. He had been squatting on forty acres when John Butterfield had made him the offer to run the stage stop. It was money and privacy, most of the time. Keep the horses fed and groomed, change the teams when the stages came through. He still talked to himself a little in between times; he talked even less when people came by asking a lot of fool questions.

Peeker and Rawlings dismounted and bulled Willits to the wall, then tied his hands behind his back with leather thongs. They ran him inside the adobe and shoved him in his bunk.

"Don't move or say anything," Peeker ordered. "We won't be long."

Outside, Bodine stood at the open door of the tack shed, his eyes scanning the small room. Rafe stood just behind him. Nearby, Culhane was shaking out a rope to catch up some fresh horses from the corral—but the choice was poor.

Bodine saw what he was looking for and stepped inside the shed, where Willits kept a small forge and tools for blacksmithing. Bodine picked up a heavy maul and a chisel. He handed them to Rafe.

"Knock these irons off me."

Bodine stepped to the anvil and placed one wrist on

the flat plane, angling it so the chisel could be set at the weakest point of the manacles.

"Might get some skin," Rafe said.

"You just see that maul don't slip."

Rafe worked the manacle into position and placed the chisel snug against the metal. He shortened up on the maul, took aim, and swung. Once, twice, a third time. The clanking filled the stable.

Peeker came inside. "Willits is tied up out of the way, Rafe. Culhane's switching saddles."

"You keep a lookout for troopers or a posse," Bodine ordered, grimacing as the manacles tore at his wrist.

"I take my orders from Rafe Adams," Peeker said belligerently.

Bodine fixed him with a stare. Rafe held the maul steady in mid-swing.

"Not anymore, you don't," said Bodine. "Only one boss of this outfit. You don't like it, you ride outa here."

Peeker looked questioningly at Rafe, who said quietly, "You keep a lookout." Peeker snorted and turned on his heel.

Rafe smashed the maul down hard, and the first manacle split apart. Bodine's wrist went numb as tiny droplets of blood oozed from the scraped skin.

"Dust cloud!"

Peeker's shadow filled the doorway of the adobe.

Bodine, rubbing both wrists with salve from a container on Willits's shelf, turned to face Peeker. "How far?"

"Mile and moving fast. More'n a half-dozen horses, I figger."

"Damn!" said Rafe. "We better light outa here."

"Hell, they'd run us down like rabbits," Bodine sneered. "Peeker, you get Willits and bring him to the door. Rafe, you and Culhane set up in the stable. Rawlings, you get down behind that big rock over to the right. Peeker and I will hold 'em off here. Let 'em get close, and don't fire until I drop a man . . . then only shoot when you can make it count."

Peeker wrestled Willits to the door as the others left to take up their positions.

"You stand just outside the door, Willits," Bodine instructed as he cut free the stationmaster's hands. "We'll have rifles aimed on your back. Whoever comes up, you just act real friendly and tell 'em you ain't seen hide nor hair of us. Savvy?"

Willits nodded, and Bodine shoved him through the door.

"I'm right behind you, Willits. Just stay right there and watch your tongue."

Bodine motioned Peeker to a position at one window, then took a place well back in the shadows of the doorway. The sun was setting and the light was fading. Anyone riding up would see only Willits outside. Now Bodine could hear the drum of hoofbeats. He saw the blue and yellow guidon flapping in the breeze, and cursed under his breath. This was no posse coming, but troopers from Fort Bliss. As he watched, the detachment came to a halt. The horses stood in formation in a column of twos. One of the soldiers lifted a spyglass to his eye; Bodine could just make out officer's bars on the man's shoulders. He didn't move a muscle. Though he was hidden in the shadowed doorway, a sharp eye might detect movement.

"Wave at them, Willits," Bodine husked. "Smile real big and wave the bastards in."

Willits waved at the troopers, and the officer put the glass away and barked an order. His words could not be heard, but the troopers broke out of column ranks and formed a skirmish line. They approached the way station slowly, their horses at a trained walk.

Bodine counted a dozen. Bad odds, but he knew the troopers were carrying single-shot, muzzle-loading carbines. The gunpowder and bullets would be loaded, but for safety the percussion caps that ignited the charge would not be set in place until an order was given. The soldiers had sidearms, but they were carried in flapped holsters on the wrong side, so that a man had to draw across his belly.

"Tell 'em to come on in, Willits. Tell 'em everything is okay."

Willits raised his arm, beckoning to the troopers. "Come ahead!" he shouted.

The lieutenant barked another order and the troopers fell back into column formation.

Bodine grinned. As he cocked the .50-caliber rifle, which he had found in the station, he held the trigger back so that there wasn't an audible click. The troopers rode forward briskly, as if relieved to find Willits there—alive.

Bodine stepped away from the line of sight in the doorway and took up a position at the left window. He looked at Peeker and nodded. Peeker, who had not yet looked out through the window, flattened himself against the wall. Bodine did the same.

"Willits?" the officer inquired.

"I'm Willits. Orville Willits."

"I'm under orders from Fort Bliss. Hunting some men—Ernie Bodine and three or four others. Perhaps more."

"No sign of 'em, Captain."

"Lieutenant."

"I'm just waitin' for the stage, Lieutenant. And it's a mite late."

"It's coming. Mind if we water our horses and stretch our legs?"

"Set down, Lieutenant, make yourself at home."

Bodine waited until he heard the order, then the creak of leather as men climbing out of their saddles put weight on the stirrups.

He ducked under the window and came up on the other side, motioning for Peeker to do the same at his window. Rising slowly, Bodine peered around the open window until he found a target. The lieutenant was looking toward the corrals. In another second he would see the saddled horses and put two and two together. Bodine slid the barrel of the rifle up, the muzzle flush with the window. He took aim, caressed the single trigger. He drew a breath and held it. Then he squeezed the trigger. The percussion cap ignited seventy grains of black powder, propelling the round ball through the rifled barrel. The lieutenant turned in surprise, but the ball caught him in the neck. The officer went down like a beheaded chicken, his body writhing reflexively. He was still alive, but the rush of blood formed a pool in the dust. Peeker's shot followed almost simultaneously, and another trooper went down, a hole in his back.

White smoke filled the air around the front of the adobe. Troopers clawed for leather holster flaps, while others yanked short Enfields from rifle scabbards on their saddles.

Rawlings, Culhane, and Adams opened deadly fire with single-shot rifles of heavy caliber. Troopers went down as if struck by grapeshot. Willits sprawled on the ground, covering his head.

Bodine lay the rifle against the wall and drew his pistol. Through the swirl of smoke, he found targets. Caps exploded, fast-burning powder ignited, balls thunked into flesh and bone. Shouts and curses filled the air as the troopers tried to return fire. A horse went down, and a soldier scrambled away from it. Disorganized, confused, the troopers fired at shadows and at flashes from pistols. They had no visible targets and, in the open, were at the mercy of the ambushers.

Peeker shot a charging trooper in the face with his Colt Navy pistol. The soldier slammed into the adobe wall, smearing it with blood. Bodine saw Adams and Culhane rush the troopers, hunched over, pistols firing. Rawlings came out from cover and joined in the pincer attack. A ball whistled through the open door of the adobe and spanged against a hanging skillet.

Then, suddenly, the firing stopped. And a terrible silence rose up on the killing ground.

Willits slowly uncovered his head and looked around. He stood up, weak kneed, weaving. Bodine stepped from the adobe and shot him in the back. Willits turned, looked at Bodine in wonder. His mouth opened in surprise, but no sound came out. He pitched forward, face down on the ground, his gasping mouth sucking in granules of dirt until his throat rattled like seeds in a dry gourd.

As soon as the shooting was over, the outlaws began to reload. Bodine cleared the last split percussion cap from his pistol and fished a powder flask from his hip pocket. He pressed the lever, holding his thumb over the spout, and filled each cylinder with an exact measurement of powder in grains. From a pouch, he poured out six over-size .44-caliber balls and placed them, one at a time, in the cylinders, tamping each one down with the ramrod so that it fit snug. He smeared each ball with tallow from a snuffbox to prevent the gun from chain firing, and then set the percussion caps on the nipples of each cylinder.

While the others were still reloading, Bodine stalked among the dead and dying soldiers. If he saw movement, he cocked his pistol and fired a ball into the head of the man.

"Stack these bodies in the barn," Bodine called to the men. "Round up those horses that didn't run off. We'll take the best along with us so we can change horses when we have to."

Adams, Culhane, Peeker, and Rawlings lugged the troopers' bodies into the barn and stacked them there like cordwood. Bodine dragged Willits by the heels and dumped him with the rest. They returned from the barn lugging the soldiers' gun belts, which they slung from the saddle horns of their horses.

"We got some extra horses, Bodine," said Culhane. "Want to bring a string?"

"No, just one extra horse to a man. Can't afford to waste ammo, so slit the throats of the rest. I don't want there to be any fresh mounts when that posse gets here."

"You think there'll be a posse with the army coming and all?" Rafe asked.

The light was fading. The hill darkened, and the ocotillos stood like the shadows of frozen men. A night-hawk whipped by overhead.

Bodine looked down the road and nodded. "They'll come—and one of them may be coming now. Look."

All of the men turned. In the distance, a pale, wraithlike funnel of dust hung over the darkening road, raised by the hooves of Lieutenant Horatio Stack's horse.

"Mount up," said Bodine. "Could be nothing. I figger just one rider put up that dust."

In moments, they were riding, each leading a spare horse. Pistols flapped from saddle horns, loaded rifles rode in scabbards. They had plenty of powder and ball, and a lone rider wasn't going to keep them from reaching Cookes Pass or stop them from capturing Vernon Blaine's daughter, Chastity.

Bodine's gut was empty, but that's the way he liked it. A hungry man made a better hunter and could run faster than a man with a belly full of beans.

He just hoped that lone rider wasn't Luke Faraday. There was a man who wouldn't give up, wouldn't stop.

Ernie Bodine smiled in the dark. Whoever was back there would need a change of mount, and all he'd find at Cottonwoods Station was fodder for the wolves and coyotes.

Chapter 3

"**W**illits ought to have a light on up ahead," Morty Tubbs drawled. "Unless he gave us up for good."

Luke Faraday held a sawed-off Greener shotgun lightly in his hands, but he could cock both barrels quickly if the need arose. They had been driving slowly for the past few miles in darkness so complete that it was a wonder Tubbs could see the road. Shortly before dark they had come upon the stolen stagecoach, the dead outlaw inside already beginning to stink, and they had stayed long enough to bury him. Afterward, it had still been light enough for the passengers to claim their belongings, but they'd had to light torches to pack the luggage boot and top carrier. Clouds had scudded in, blotting out the stars, and the moon had not yet risen.

Luke had been disappointed but not surprised upon discovering that the outlaws had taken his sorrel gelding with them when they had abandoned the stolen stage. He took some solace, however, in the fact that they had not found his Hawken rifle in the fringed buckskin case, which they had left behind on the roof of the stage.

"Even if he isn't expecting us, the eastbound's about due," Luke noted.

"I reckon. Well, we got a coupla miles yet. Damn, we ought sure to see a light by now, 'less'n Orville's snakebit or drinkin' to cure it in advance.'' Morty spat a stream of tobacco juice from the corner of his mouth. It disappeared in the inky darkness, but someone inside the coach protested at an open window.

Morty cackled, rattling the reins. Hell, they were five or six hours late now, but the mail was aboard and the passengers had all their baggage. Troopers were out after Bodine, and the air was heavy with the promise of rain—or at least some coolness after a sweltering day under a hammering sun.

Merle Jenkins wiped the tobacco juice off the back of his hand with his sleeve. A lantern inside the coach threw an uncertain flickering light over the faces of the passengers—faces that seemed to appear and disappear as the shadows danced. The lantern's cloying odor was intensified by the smell of coal oil that drifted in through open windows from the outside lanterns. But dust and tobacco spray drifted in just as often.

"Damned driver," muttered Jenkins. "It's mighty poor service on Butterfield's line."

No one paid him any attention except Congressman Hiram Cornwallis, who clucked in agreement. He had scarcely touched the lunch packet provided at the last minute in El Paso. It lay open on his lap: baked chicken, soggy boiled potatoes, shriveled peaches, moistureless grapes that had become desiccated in the heat. For most of the journey he had been sneaking sips from a clear whiskey bottle. That smell, too, clung to the coach and lingered on his lips. Cornwallis made a big display out of being sneaky with the bottle, and he constantly groomed his muttonchop sideburns and bushy salt-and-pepper whiskers in between fanning himself with a magazine.

His aide, Stuart Gorman, had long since lost interest in the congressman's antics. At first Stuart had been thrilled to work for such a distinguished gentleman, but their relationship was not based on party loyalty. Gorman had obtained his position through strong family connections in the District of Columbia; his father had always dreamed of having a son who would rise to the top in politics, since he himself had been too busy acquiring wealth to devote time in service to the public.

Gorman had worked in the congressman's office only a short while—two months—and already found himself disillusioned with Washington in general and Cornwallis in particular. There were times when he questioned if the man was completely honest. He had heard some rumors and snatches of conversation that made him wonder if Cornwallis would even be in office at the end of Stuart's trial year. It was exciting to bypass being a page and to go to work directly for a congressman, but perhaps his family had moved him up the political ladder too quickly. Other young men his own age treated him with a lack of courtesy—some of them with downright hostility—and they referred to his boss as Old Walrus-Puss.

Young Gorman was not thinking of the congressman now, however. His clear blue eyes kept glancing at Chastity Blaine, who sat at the window. They were about the same age. Stuart had just turned twenty, although he did not look even that old with his short-cropped, light-brown hair, square chin, and smooth face. Once he had tried to grow a beard, but the results had been disappointing: a bit of blond fluff and amber fuzz. His lips were thin and reddish, as though he used lip rouge—a constant source of teasing from his peers.

Chastity was not aware of Stuart Gorman's interest. She looked out the window but did not see anything in the darkness. Instead, she thought of the rifled satchel she had recovered from the stolen stage: the letters that were taken, a photograph she meant to give her father when she saw him. To think of her picture and private letters in the hands of that murderer was almost too much to bear.

Lorene Martin sat opposite Chastity, but she did not look at the troubled girl. Rather, she had been observing the curious, though hidden, bond that seemed to exist between the Jenkinses and Congressman Cornwallis. There was nothing specific, nothing she could put her finger on, but her suspicions were aroused, nonetheless. It was odd. The couple acted as if they did not know Cornwallis. But

Lorene thought she detected an underlying intimacy that went beyond mere acquaintance. Anne Jenkins was a most curious woman. Light-haired and pinch-faced, she was constantly whispering in her husband's ear while directing meaningful glances at Cornwallis. She was a small nervous woman, severely dressed, with her hair up in a spinster's bun as if acknowledging that she was no beauty—inside or out.

Suddenly it occurred to Lorene why she felt as she did. It was not so much that Merle and Anne Jenkins appeared to know the congressman—it was the pains they took to avoid divulging there was some connection, however tenuous. Each time that Cornwallis looked at Merle Jenkins, the latter would turn away quickly. And Anne Jenkins was very careful never to look directly into the congressman's eyes. Quite difficult, since they were sitting exactly opposite one another!

Lorene sat up straight as she realized something else—something she had almost missed. Earlier, Merle Jenkins had scribbled something on a piece of paper and slipped it into his wife's hand. Lorene's curiosity had been aroused because Anne had not looked at the note. Instead, she had clutched it in her palm so tightly that her knuckles had turned white. Now, Lorene looked and noted that Mrs. Jenkins still had her fist closed.

The coach began to rumble along at a faster pace, despite the darkness. Normally the stage averaged four miles an hour along such a stretch, but Morty was trying to make up for lost time and drove the team hard. The wheels clattered or hummed, depending on the surface of the road. Now, as they neared Cottonwoods Station, Morty broke out the bullwhip and cracked it over the backs of the horses.

The coach lurched and the passengers were thrown from their seats.

"Oh!" exclaimed Chastity, pitching into Lorene's lap. Merle Jenkins threw out his arms to keep from landing on young Gorman. Anne was thrown toward Cornwallis. When the coach recovered, the same thing happened again, only this time Lorene found herself on top of Chastity,

Gorman wound up on the floor, while Cornwallis braced himself against Gorman to keep from barreling into Anne Jenkins.

Lorene regained her composure and smiled wanly at Chastity. The lantern swung to and fro, casting an eerie yellow light on everyone, but the flame did not go out. Lorene found herself looking at Anne's hand. The fist was no longer closed tightly. Instead, Mrs. Jenkins opened her hand and patted her hair back in place.

"Sorry," said Stuart Gorman, bumping into Lorene as he got back on his seat.

"That's all right. It's quite a rough ride."

"Yes," Anne interjected. "I suppose the stage driver is one of those incompetents hired by Mr. Butterfield."

"No," said Lorene, contradicting her. "I just think he's trying to make up for lost time."

"Damned inconsiderate if you ask me," said Merle.

"Worst trip I've ever taken," Cornwallis agreed.

Chastity looked bewildered. Lorene reached over and patted her knees. "We'll stop soon, I'm sure. Are you ill?"

"No. It's just that I'm feeling faint from being closed in this long. It's so dark outside, and those fumes are stifling. It's so dusty that one can scarcely breathe."

"I agree," Lorene nodded in sympathy.

But no one made a move to extinguish the lantern. It was as if they were all afraid of the dark.

"Young man," the congressman addressed Stuart, "I wonder if we might change places for a while? I'd like to talk to Miss Martin."

"Yes, sir," Gorman replied, not at all sure he wanted to be seated so far away from Chastity Blaine. The two exchanged seats in the lurching coach.

Lorene sat stiffly, wondering at the sudden attention from the whiskey-breath politician. As if reading her mind, he fished for a clove and placed it in his mouth. For several moments he worked the thorny spice around in his mouth, wetting it with saliva until it began to burn his tongue.

"Been wanting to speak with you, Miss Martin," he finally said, in that deep, resonant voice that orators cultivated. "I believe I saw you in Washington a time or two. Were you not in Senator John Bell's office?"

"Yes."

"You know John well?"

"No, not at all well. He's a friend of my father's."

"Ah, then that is why I know your name. Martin. Are you related to Chief Martin of San Francisco?"

Lorene was surprised that he would bring the matter up. She knew the congressman and her father had always disliked each other, and she was convinced her visit to Washington was connected with Cornwallis in some specific way. Like her father, he was from San Francisco, but he always bragged that his family was old-line Eastern with strong connections among the military. In fact, the congressman had run for office on that connection, promising more forts, more protection for emigrants, safer roads, more land, reduced taxes, and closer ties between Washington and San Francisco—none of which had he accomplished.

"Randolph Martin is my father. But you must know he is no longer chief of police."

"Of course. Retired, I believe. Fine man, fine man."

"He's in private practice," said Lorene, curious now why the politician would pursue such dangerous ground. When her father was head of the police, he publicly denounced Cornwallis as a thief. At that time, there were rumors that the congressman had lined his own pockets through various shady land deals. But nothing was ever proven, and the talk eventually died down.

Yet since her father's retirement, men had come to their home who were from Washington. And Cornwallis's name had been mentioned more than once. Lately her father had been unusually reticent to speak about Cornwallis in public, but she suspected that her trip to Washington was concerned with an official investigation being conducted by him.

She had been asked to deliver a packet to Senator John K. Bell and wait for a return packet. The packet was not large and fit neatly into her hand-carried carpetbag. Now, talking to Cornwallis, she was curious about the packet's contents and almost considered opening it. Yet she pushed the thought away; she would never violate her father's trust in her. Senator Bell had stressed its importance when he gave it to her; she remembered his exact words: "This will make your father very happy, my dear. This will give him the ammunition he needs to bring an old adversary to justice."

Her thoughts were brought to a sudden halt as Morty Tubbs hauled in on the reins and the coach rumbled to an abrupt stop.

Chastity stuck her head out the window beside her. Jenkins and Gorman both did the same on the opposite side of the coach. "Why, it appears we've arrived at the stage station," she said.

Lorene could see only blackness outside. But there was a heavy dampness in the air and a sudden coolness that was refreshing.

"You all just stay put," Morty said in a loud whisper. "Don't anybody get out of the coach."

The passengers drew together and spoke in low tones, speculating on why they were not allowed to get out and stretch.

"Damned quiet," Faraday remarked to Tubbs.

"I don't like it. Willits ought to be out here waving a lantern. The adobe's dark, too."

Morty's hand touched the butt of his holstered pistol. Something was wrong. The cottonwoods were dark and it was ghostly quiet. There was the cloying scent of death in the air.

"Step down easy," Luke told Tubbs. "I'll take a look around."

Both men climbed down.

Inside the coach, Cornwallis snorted. "I'm getting out," he said. He stepped past Lorene and Chastity, flipped the latch, and swung the door open. He climbed down and straightened his jacket. "What is this place, driver?" he asked.

"The Cottonwoods," said Morty.

Luke came around the Concord and saw Cornwallis. Light from the coach illuminated both men.

"You follow orders, same as everyone else here," said Faraday. "Get back inside the coach."

"I'll have you know . . ."

"Move!" Luke pushed the politician roughly, forcing him back inside the coach.

"Unhand me!" Cornwallis brayed.

Luke gave him a final shove, and the congressman suffered the indignity of pitching face forward between the other passengers.

"Morty," Luke said, "get that lantern out of the coach. We might need it."

Tubbs moved with alacrity. The lantern was held in a double-gimbaled cage of his own design. Many passengers appreciated the light on the night runs, even though it was not a standard item. He had gotten the idea from seeing the hurricane lamps aboard sailing ships in New Orleans. The double gimbal forced the lantern to hang steady no matter which way the coach pitched. He slipped the lantern from its holder.

"What's wrong?" asked Chastity.

"Maybe nothing," Tubbs replied. "You just sit tight until Luke checks things out."

Luke took the lantern from the driver. Holding it in his left hand, he started walking toward the adobe, his right hand palming the butt of his Colt.

It was deathly quiet. Dark splotches on the ground drew his attention. He knelt down, holding the lamp high, then touched the gritty stain and smelled it on the tip of his finger. Dried blood, and plenty of it. Something was wrong. One man could not have spilled so much blood. It was everywhere in front of the adobe, and he spotted drag marks, a roil of footprints and hoofprints. Earlier, there had been men and horses here—a dozen or so, from the tracks.

Luke made his way to the stable, following the drag marks—blood drips that had dried but left a telltale path. The stench of death grew stronger.

A sudden scream froze Luke in his tracks. It was full of anguish, fear, terror. His blood turned chill, and the hackles rose on the back of his neck. Quickly, he went into a crouch and drew his .44, cocking it as it cleared the holster.

A trooper appeared at the stable door, clutching his bloody head. He moaned, staggering toward the bounty hunter.

Luke holstered his pistol and set the lantern down.

"I—I'm shot! And—they're all dead in there!"

The trooper was young, in his late teens or early twenties.

"Steady, son," Luke said, holding the lad up. "What happened here?"

"We was ambushed. Didn't see 'em. They killed the lieutenant, and the bullets was flyin'—blood everywhere. God, I thought I was dead when I come to!"

"You're not hurt bad," said Luke, lifting the lantern so the light could shine on the head wound. "A crease."

Morty came running over from the stage. Following him were Lorene and young Gorman.

"Take care of him, Morty," said Luke. "I'll see if there's any more alive in there."

"Let me take a look at that wound," Lorene said. "Can we get some hot water?"

"Might be I could light the stove in the adobe," Morty offered.

Gorman helped Lorene hold the soldier up as the three of them headed for the adobe, while Luke carried the lantern inside the stable. There he saw a sight of such horror that his knees buckled. The horses had been butchered—heads caved in with a bloodied ax, throats burst open from the same deadly instrument. A senseless waste of horseflesh.

And then he saw the soldiers, piled in a grotesque heap, a tangle of arms and legs, with eyes staring blankly into eternity. Orville Willits lay face down, a hole in his back. The carnage was sickening, beyond any horror Faraday had ever seen. A pathetic slaughter of good men, shot down without warning.

He forced himself to go through the pile. Rigor mortis had set in, and the bodies were oddly angled in frozen positions. No one else was alive. He saw where someone had shot them in the heads to make sure. Bodine! The bastard had waited for them in ambush and cut them down with no mercy. Luke's teeth ground down in anger. The troopers had been stripped of arms and ammo pouches. Here and there was a paper cartridge, gunpowder spilling onto the ground. So Bodine and his bunch had carbines and plenty of ball and powder. And horses, probably two per man. Bodine could travel far and fast.

Faraday wished for a horse now. His own was not among those slaughtered, and he was grateful for that. The sorrel gelding was a good mount, with plenty of bottom and deep lungs. Bodine knew the horse—it had tracked him to the Huecos—and it galled Luke to think the outlaw was probably riding him right now. Well, that made him not just a murderer, but a horse thief as well, and that alone was a hanging offense anywhere in the West, where wealth often was measured by the numbers and kinds of horses a man possessed. Bodine had a lot to answer for, and Luke aimed to see he paid in hard coin.

Faraday left the stable and headed to the adobe, where he found the passengers making use of the big dining room and lounge. Lanterns had been lighted, and Chastity was helping Anne Jenkins fix supper. Cornwallis was napping in a chair while Merle Jenkins fidgeted at a table, listening to Morty talk to the wounded soldier. Lorene had cleaned the young trooper's wound and was now dressing it with salve and a fresh bandage she had found in a cabinet. Luke set the lantern down on a bench and strode to the corner where Morty stood watching Lorene.

"Get anything out of him, Morty?"

Morty shook his head. "Kid's mighty scairt. Can't make much sense out of his tale."

"Let me try. Excuse me, miss," he said as he knelt beside Lorene and the trooper.

"My name's Lorene Martin, Mr. Faraday."

"My friends call me Luke. How's the lad?"

"In shock mostly. He said he was buried under some dead men. The wound isn't bad—the bullet only skimmed his skull, tore loose some skin."

Luke knelt and looked into the trooper's eyes. "What's your name, son? I'm Luke Faraday."

The boy focused on Luke, and he seemed to calm. His eyes steadied, narrowed. "They're all dead, ain't they?"

Luke nodded. "You're not hurt bad. At least not outside. Can you tell me what happened? It would help if I knew your name."

"Ned. Ned Cooper. They were waiting for us. Bodine's bunch, I reckon. I know who you are. You brought him in. Should have shot him, that's what you should have done."

"Steady. Did you see Bodine?"

Cooper shook his head.

"Don't move so much," said Lorene. "I'm almost finished. This ought to help."

She split the bandage expertly and tied it neatly. Luke watched her, admiring her flame hair, the way the light spun gold and copper all through it. Her eyes startled him when she looked up. They were open, flashing emerald— the kind of eyes that could melt a man inside, make his stomach boil with butterflies.

"Go on," said Luke. "Get it off your chest, trooper."

"We was all gettin' off our horses. Willits was standin' out there sayin' it was all right, and then the lieutenant went down. I saw Sergeant Hooper take a ball in the shoulder, and then we tried to get the Enfields out. The firin' seemed to come from all directions. We couldn't see no one. There was so much smoke, and they was usin' big-bore muskets or rifles—.58 caliber, at least. Then they started into us with pistols. I got hit and everythin' turned black. I felt someone fall on me, and when I woke up I was under a pile—of bodies. I didn't know what it was at first till I felt somebody's face and an arm, all stiffened up like stove wood. I close to died in there from pure bein' scairt."

Luke stood up and patted Ned's shoulder. "You did fine, soldier. Anybody'd be scared in the same situation. Did you see Lieutenant Stack? He isn't among the dead."

"Nope. I know the lieutenant, but we never saw him."

Merle Jenkins rose from the table where he had been sitting, staring at the back of the adobe's door. He walked over to it and tore a scrap of paper that had been tacked there. "Seems Stack was by here," he announced. "Left this note."

Tubbs and Faraday walked over and read the note Jenkins was holding.

Passed by, saw what Bodine did. Will send a burial crew from Fort Fillmore. I am in pursuit. It was signed: *Lt. Horatio Stack, U.S. Cavalry.*

"Fort Fillmore's eighteen miles," said Tubbs.

"He won't get much help at Fillmore," Ned Cooper replied, standing up on shaky legs. Lorene reached out for him, but he brushed her away. He walked over to Faraday, getting steadier with every step.

"What do you mean?" asked Luke.

"Heard it at Bliss. Orders went out yesterday to send most of the Fillmore detachment to Fort Defiance in the north. Indian troubles."

"Indians?" Morty almost swallowed his cud of tobacco.

"Apache."

"It'll be fully light in an hour," Morty said as he walked from the stagecoach to where Luke was standing, near the way-station building.

"Yeah. Couldn't sleep. Horses rested enough?"

"Have to be. I checked that squeaky hub on that patched-up wheel. It's okay for now, but it may need some more greasing before we reach Yuma."

It had been Luke's decision to stay over at Cotton-woods Station to rest the horses and let the passengers and Ned Cooper get some sleep. There were other decisions to be made. Luke had slept little himself, but he felt alert, keyed up. Bodine was somewhere ahead. Still unanswered was what had happened to the overdue eastbound stage from Yuma. Indians? . . . Or Bodine again? Bodine apparently was headed for Yuma, either to break out his partner, Chet Morgan, or to dig up the payroll he'd buried before he and Morgan had been captured. There was another man with him, who Luke suspected might have been in on the payroll robbery. Luke had seen the man who drove the stolen stage out of El Paso, and it was the same man who was on a poster they had found in the adobe. And the poster said this Rafe Adams had worked in army payroll disbursing in San Francisco—the perfect spot for an inside man.

"We got the pass to go through," said Faraday. "Worries me that Bodine might know who the girl is—Chastity Blaine."

"Think he might try to get her? Use her to spring Morgan?"

"It's a point to think about. His taking those letters and her picture makes me think Bodine would pull something like that if he thought he could get away with it. He's a desperate man. What he did to those soldiers and to the horses gives me a whole new eyeful of the man."

"I'll hitch up the team," said Morty. "Gawdamighty, you give a man a heap to worry over."

"Mr. Faraday . . . Luke . . ." whispered Lorene Martin as he started back to the adobe to rouse the passengers. She stepped out of the shadows. She smelled of soap and powder and flowery perfume.

"Yes?"

"I—I didn't know until now, but it seems Ned Cooper left about an hour ago. Jenkins and Cornwallis are bragging about it—seems they convinced Ned to set out for Fort Bliss on foot, seeing as how he said we wouldn't get any help from Fort Fillmore."

"On foot?!"

"Cornwallis is droning on about how he thinks you've assumed too much authority. Apparently they convinced Ned it was his responsibility as a soldier to go for help. Then they gave him canteens and snuck him out the back."

With a furious oath, Luke stormed into the adobe, his anger a surging current in his veins.

Jenkins was waiting for him. "You're not in command here, Faraday! It's too late to stop Cooper. He *wanted* to go for help. We acted in the best interests of all concerned."

Luke glared at them—Anne Jenkins, Cornwallis, Merle Jenkins. Chastity woke up on the divan, rubbed sleep from her eyes. It was obvious she had nothing to do with Cooper's leaving.

"You've probably sent him to his death," Luke said, his fury subsiding. Jenkins was a stupid, self-centered man. It would be like clubbing a dummy to strike him—hardly worth the effort.

"When we get to San Francisco, Mr. Faraday," Anne announced, "we're going to file a full report and recommend that you and Mr. Tubbs never be allowed near a stage line again. You've kept us in this deathly place all night, refused to bury the dead, and put us all in danger."

It was no use explaining to her that the horses needed rest and that the army had to see their dead for themselves. Her pinched face seemed even more weasellike, and he felt the lash of her hatred.

"You do what you wish, ma'am. Now board the stage. And pray you all *get* to San Francisco."

As if to punctuate his words, a terrible scream floated to them from far away, cutting the predawn air like something unreal, ghostly.

Chapter 4

Lorene looked at Luke, her green eyes wide with fear. She drew a hand to her throat. Just then Stuart Gorman came in through the back door. He had been outside, relieving himself.

The scream came to them again, even more terrifying than before, jellying their blood, rippling their flesh with goosebumps.

"Who is it?" asked Gorman, his face blanched.

"That's Cooper!" Luke shouted, bolting for the door.

Lorene sidestepped to avoid being bowled over. As Luke rushed outside, he saw Morty running from the corral where the horses had been grained.

"Get 'em hitched, Morty!" yelled Luke. "We may have to get out of here in a hurry."

"What in the name of Jehoshaphat was that?"

Luke scrambled onto the stage and jerked his Hawken rifle from its sheath. Standing on the driver's platform, he detached the ramrod and cleaned the barrel as quickly as his hands would allow. Then he lifted the powder horn that was slung across his chest. The horn had a brass spout. By holding his fingertip over it and pressing a release button, a premeasured amount of black powder filled the spout. He had it set at eighty grains, but he could judge it to one hundred ten or cut it back to fifty for small game, sixty to seventy for close shots on larger animals. He loaded eighty grains down the barrel, then took a strip of ticking patch from his bag and a round bullet slightly smaller than the barrel. He spit on the patch, placed the ball on it over the muzzle, and pushed it partially down with the short end of a barrel starter. Then he cut the excess patch and rammed the ball down farther with the long end of the starter. Finally, he rammed the ball home with the ramrod, seating it solidly on the powder.

He cocked the rifle, fitted a percussion cap on the nipple under the hammer, and climbed from the driver's seat up onto the roof of the coach, sprawling on the luggage with the Hawken resting on the rear rail.

The passengers drifted from the adobe as a pale line of light appeared on the eastern horizon.

"Luke?" It was Lorene. She stood below, looking up at him.

"Yeah?"

"Can I help? I can shoot."

"Stay close to the adobe. Get inside if there's shooting."

"What do you think it is?"

"I don't know."

But he knew. A man didn't scream like that unless he was being tortured beyond endurance. That wasn't a scream of fear. It was a scream that told of pain so deep it became part of the mind and flesh. Hard pain. The kind of pain that would make a man go over the edge, even to the point of killing himself—any way he could.

The light spread over the eastern horizon like a cream stain. The low rocky hills became defined. A high butte turned a faint peach, then bronzed as the sun struck it directly. The land slowly took on light as if struck by a firebrand at some distant point.

Lorene looked around and saw the tattered guidon near the stable. Shot pouches and powder flasks that had been invisible in the dark became recognizable as the light spread rapidly. A pistol lay against a stump, and the stock of a rifle, overlooked by the fleeing outlaws, could be seen close to the adobe.

"I—I'm going to help," she told Luke, who nodded absentmindedly. His eyes strained to see in the distance, to determine shapes that were not saguaro or prickly pear.

The sun climbed into a cobalt sky without a single speck to mar its clarity, but still he saw nothing. No sign. Only a silence that rose up from the sun-glazed land—a silence that deepened with every passing moment.

Stuart Gorman stepped away from the travelers clustered at the door of the adobe and walked over to where Lorene was picking up arms and ammunition. He watched her in fascination as she handled an 1858 model army revolver, deftly checking its cylinders. She lifted a rifle in her hands and saw that it was loaded and capped.

"Here, you keep the pistol for me," she told Gorman, "in case I need it later."

"You would shoot someone with these?"

"If I was forced to."

"Yes," he said. "I suppose I could, too."

Soon they saw the dust—a thin cloud of it rising slowly in the dawn air.

Luke rose up slightly, as if trying to look over the rise beyond the cottonwoods. "Someone's coming!" he said. "Take cover!"

With the dust came the yells—hawking cries that sounded at first like faraway shouts of children playing. As they drew closer, they became bloodcurdling whoops that ripped through the silence like the flapping of battle flags in the wind.

A man ran over the top of the hill, into view.

Luke steadied his finger on the trigger. The hill was out of rifle range, but Ned Cooper was clearly recognizable now in his blue, yellow-striped trousers. His shirt was off, and his cap flew away as he came running down the hill.

Stuart Gorman started to run toward the soldier.

"Don't!" commanded Faraday.

"But he's hurt! Someone's chasing him!"

"Steady down, son. Can't you hear them? Apaches!"

Morty finished the last hookup of the horses. "Stage's ready to roll!" he announced.

"Get 'em aboard!" Luke shouted.

Just then Ned Cooper stopped and turned around. It was plain to see he was breathing hard, struggling for his breath.

As the passengers watched, six Apache braves swooped over the rise and raced their horses straight for the soldier. They carried war clubs, and rifle butts poked out of scabbards. Dressed in colorful, loose-fitting clothes, headbands bright in the sun, two warriors converged on Cooper, swinging their clubs. Expertly, they struck the youth from either side.

Cooper screamed in pain as he tried to lift a hand to touch the other arm.

"Jesus," said Morty. "They broke both his arms."

"Get those people ready!" shouted Luke.

The passengers stared in horror at the swarming Apaches, who now were showing off, riding circles around Cooper, striking him at will as he staggered, trying to avoid the bone-crushing blows from the war clubs. The young trooper fell, then rose up as two warriors rode dazzlingly close and nicked him with lances—just the tips—pricking the skin until blood flowed.

They let Cooper stumble down the hill, closer to the stage stop. The Indians seemed to be disorganized, unsure of themselves, but Luke knew different. They were waiting—measuring the distance. Again, that awful silence, so deep it filled a man's ear with a sound like an underwater river at floodtide . . . a huge, roaring silence that shrieked in the brain.

Cooper stumbled, regained his footing, and staggered on, blood streaming from tiny slits in his chest. Luke saw his face then—contorted, waxen, his eyes wide with an awesome fear.

The Apaches struck again. In pairs.

This time, they attacked with knives, leaning over the sides of their mounts, slashing as they burst past the startled and bewildered trooper. Blades flashing in the sun, they struck with precision. Cooper screamed and lashed out blindly, but as quickly as each Indian struck, he was gone, replaced by another attacker.

Chastity went into hysterics, screaming and babbling until Stuart had to clamp his hand over her mouth and drag her to the coach, where she could no longer see the horror. Anne Jenkins shrieked in terror and fled to the confines of the Concord, Merle trailing after her, helpless, angry.

"Aren't you going to do anything?" he shouted up at Faraday.

"Mister, this is sport to them. You see a half-dozen braves. There are three times that number you can't see."

Cornwallis could no longer look up the slope. He, too, scrambled into the coach. Morty stood by, the shotgun cocked.

Lorene climbed up to the driver's seat and lay alongside Faraday, steadying her rifle on her shoulder.

"You don't belong here," he said gruffly.

"I can cover you and give you time to reload," she said. "They may charge."

"I reckon not. They're having fun with young Cooper. When it's over, they'll go back to camp and brag like hell." He hoped she couldn't read the doubt in his voice.

"You know them?"

"Apaches. No one knows 'em much."

"But you . . . you almost seem to admire them."

"They do what they believe in doing. They don't know any better. Their ways are their ways, same as ours are ours."

Lorene forced herself to look at Cooper. He was close now, and the Indians had withdrawn slightly. Cooper, his mouth bloodied, his chest streaked with crimson, was struggling to run. The braves were shouting, cawing like crows chasing an owl.

Then, a lone Apache burst from the pack and swooped down on Cooper, his pinto pony a blur of black and white and brown. He reined in hard, leaped from the back of his pony, and flashed a knife. *Swish, swish.*

Cooper's throat was cut from ear to ear. Yet the blade tip had gone only deep enough to draw blood—not enough to finish the job.

Luke raised his rifle as the lone warrior rode back to the pack of Indians. "Now they'll come!" he said, taking aim.

Confused, grasping his throat, Cooper lost his sense of direction. He staggered aimlessly in a circle, then started back upslope. The Apaches gave a mighty roar in unison and charged.

Luke's Hawken boomed. Smoke and flame burst from the .50-caliber muzzle.

Ned Cooper's head jerked as the bullet struck the back of his skull. His legs held him for a moment, then he collapsed.

The warriors drew up, angered.

Faraday stood up, brandishing his rifle. He shouted, and Lorene's blood froze. The cry was more savage than the Apaches'. More horrible. More chilling.

The Indians turned as one and whipped their ponies to the top of the rise. And disappeared.

Lorene looked at Luke, her green eyes cloudy with puzzlement. "Why?" she breathed. "Why?"

Morty, already climbing up to take his seat, could see the pain in Luke's and Lorene's eyes, and he answered, "Because that boy had suffered enough in this world, lady. And they would have stuck him on the end of a lance and drove him straight down here just so's they could gloat about it over the campfire tonight. Now get on down in that coach—we're pullin' out!"

Lieutenant Horatio Stack had long since lost track of the time, but he figured it had to be past midnight as he wearily stood at attention in Captain Quentin Freedley's office at Fort Fillmore, twenty miles northwest of Cottonwoods Station.

"I find your story hard to believe, Lieutenant," the pompous captain droned on. "No word has reached me from Fort Bliss. Nor have we seen this man Bodine and his cohorts passing this way. Rather, it was a night patrol that found you, wandering around on a lathered horse, without orders or provisions. My instincts tell me that you are probably a deserter—a deserter who got caught and made up this cock-and-bull story.''

Stack tried his best to remain at attention. His mouth was parched from thirst, even though he'd been given water until he choked on it. His uniform was filthy; the pores of his skin were caked with dust; his legs no longer had any feeling in them. For the past ten minutes he had listened to Captain Freedley ask him dozens of questions about his post and duties without ever hearing anything the lieutenant had said about Bodine's escape.

"Surely, sir, you must know that Bodine was to be sent back to Yuma to hang. I assure you that I am in pursuit, and the reason you have had no dispatch from Fort Bliss is that a detachment was slaughtered at Cottonwoods Station—to a man.''

Freedley harrumphed for the hundredth time and moved a toy cannon across his desk. He was an arrogant boor who resented being transferred to Fort Fillmore, a desolate outpost in the heart of Indian country.

"I urge you to send a rider to Fort Bliss to confirm my story,'' Stack continued.

"Confirm? Confirm your poppycock? You tell me that this Bodine and three or four other men killed a patrol of a dozen trained cavalrymen? You, who almost killed your horse, an act of indecency no cavalry officer would perpetrate . . . you have the gall to insist I swallow such a story?''

"Check it out, sir. I ask only for provisions and a fresh horse so that I may continue my pursuit of Bodine. I lost men, too, during the escape.''

Freedley shoved the toy cannon straight toward the edge of his desk and stood up, his corpulent bulk shadowing the territorial map on the wall.

"I have no men to send to Fort Bliss. I have been stripped bare. Do you understand? Stripped to the bone because of these damnable savages. Apaches. First here, then there—like smoke. And now that crazy Mangas is on the loose somewhere, stirring up every little Apache band from El Paso to the Gila River. No, sir, I cannot spare men to ride off in the night on a wild goose chase. Instead, sir, if you are indeed an officer in the United States Army, I ask you to stand at house arrest until the stage comes through from El Paso. Dismissed.''

Stack sagged, caught himself, and saluted. Freedley ignored the salute and turned his back on the officer.

"The corporal will show you to quarters, Stack," he mumbled.

The lieutenant stumbled along behind a corporal to a sod shack that was little more than a cell. "This is officer's quarters?" he asked.

"Detention hut, sir. Sorry."

Stack listened to the bolt slam shut. It was pitch dark inside the hut. He groped and found the cot. Then he lay down, without undressing, and sank into sleep like something that has been hammered and melted in the baking sun until there no longer is any shape or form to it.

Lieutenant Stack struggled up from the depths of sleep, through overlapping layers of dream and consciousness. A voice rasped against his eardrum; hands shook his shoulders.

"Reveille, Lieutenant. Captain Freedley wants to see you."

"Huh?" Stack rubbed his eyes and sat up. The room now had shape and definition: a pair of high windows, a cot, a table, dirt floor, a broken chair.

"Stage got in from El Paso, sir," the private explained. "The story's all over the fort. You'd better double-time it to the captain's quarters."

Fifteen minutes later, the seedy-looking lieutenant stood beside Morty Tubbs and Luke Faraday in Captain Quentin Freedley's bedroom. The captain was still buttoning his shirt, and his aide-de-camp stood at nervous attention beside the bed.

"It appears your story has substance," said Freedley,

reaching into a bowl on the bed and plopping a grape into his pudgy mouth. "However, since you have no signed orders . . ."

"Begging your pardon, sir, I was responsible for Bodine. It's my responsibility to get him back. Sir . . ."

"That is all, Lieutenant. I can order you back to your post at Fort Bliss, but I am merely going to suggest that you return at once. In the meantime, you'll find a fresh horse saddled and waiting, the sutler shop open for your provisions, and a hot meal in the officers' mess."

"Sir, are you saying that—?"

"I'm saying nothing, Stack! You just get your ass out of here and don't kill that horse!"

Stack grinned sheepishly. Morty winked at him. Luke smiled and saluted with two fingers.

"Impetuous bastard," Freedley muttered after Stack had left. "He'll follow Bodine, of course. Wish I could spare some men. From what you've told me, Bodine ought to be stood to the wall and shot summarily."

"Summarily," cackled Tubbs. "Right in the—"

"Captain," Faraday interrupted, in a serious tone. "We need fresh stage horses and a couple of saddle horses for spares."

Freedley moved to the edge of his bed, lifting the bowl of grapes onto his lap. He raised a stockinged foot, and his aide brought over a boot and began slipping it on. The bed sagged under Freedley's considerable weight, yet it would never have occurred to him that this was one reason he had been assigned to Fort Fillmore.

"I can spare you two horses. You'll have to do with those. Faraday, what kind of a man slaughters horses with an ax?"

"Bodine's kind. There are such men in the West. Few, perhaps, but just one is like a sore that won't heal up. You have to cut it out, burn it dead, or the whole body decays."

"Yes, I see your point. Gentlemen, I thank you for your report on the Apaches—they are far closer than I had thought. You figure a band of twenty or thirty?"

"We counted a dozen or so," said Tubbs, "but there was more, sneakin' around out there."

"Any idea of the tribe?"

Morty shook his head.

"Mimbreño," Faraday said quietly.

"You're sure, mister?"

"I'm sure. Some of Mangas's bunch."

Freedley uttered an oath as he stamped his foot into the second boot. His aide's face turned red, and sweat popped out above his brows.

"Mangas Sangrías," Morty intoned. "Old Bleeding Sleeves."

"The name," said Luke, "means he's had his sleeves dipped in blood."

"Yes, well, if we don't stop him, the whole Southwest will be dipped in blood." Freedley stood up and snapped his suspenders. He set the grapes down on a side table, taking a small cluster in his hand. "But I can't figure out why they didn't wipe you out. Twenty of them, and only a handful of you."

"There ain't no tellin' about Apaches, Captain," offered Tubbs. "One minute they's peaceful as ducks in a pond, and the next they's flying like hawks—plumb crazy."

Luke's face hardened as a shadow flickered over his pale gray eyes. Apaches were unpredictable, it was true, but the captain had touched on something that might be important. The braves could have taken them—easily. And they knew there were women there, with only three or four guns to face at the most. Yet they had not attacked. Why?

There had to be a reason. There had to be.

An hour later, Morty Tubbs had finished greasing the patched-up wheel. "Oughta hold 'er awhile." He wiped his hands with a rag, then stored the can of grease in the boot.

The horses were hitched. He and Luke had substituted the two fresh horses provided by Captain Freedley for the lead stage horses, which they had tied to the rear of the coach.

"That wheel'll slow us down," said Morty, "but I reckon there ain't no hurry. Likely more trouble ahead, with Bodine goin' in the same direction."

"And the eastbound from Yuma is long overdue," mused Faraday.

He turned away from Morty and went to tell the passengers to board. He also wanted to offer them each a chance to stay under fort protection if they so desired. As he approached the open door of the mess hall, he stopped in his tracks, listening.

". . . If you ask me, he's just as bloodthirsty as Bodine. A most reprehensible character—not at all the caliber of man a stage company ought to hire."

It was the voice of Congressman Hiram Cornwallis, carrying past the door from where the passengers had breakfasted.

"I agree with you, Congressman," said Jenkins. "Faraday should have shot an Apache instead of that hapless soldier."

Luke walked inside, utterly calm.

Jenkins stopped talking and glared at Faraday. Cornwallis drew himself up, hands fitted to his coat as if posing for a portrait. Stuart Gorman blinked, and Chastity smiled weakly. Lorene seemed the most sympathetic to the bounty hunter. She gazed frankly at Luke, her green eyes sparkling, radiant, her hair brushed to a high sheen.

"If you want to talk about a man, Jenkins, do it to his face. That goes for you, too, Congressman."

"We were just discussing—" Cornwallis began.

"Never mind," Luke cut in, dismissing him with a wave of the hand. "Ladies, you better get aboard if you plan to go on with us. I don't advise it, but the choice is yours. Anyone who wants to stay behind until this business is cleared up, the company'll pay for it."

Stuart Gorman left hastily after Cornwallis shot him a secretive look. Chastity began gathering her purse and a small fan made of stiff paper. Lorene looked under her bench and all around her for something. A moment later, she too left. Anne Jenkins stood up and walked briskly toward the door. Deliberately, it appeared, she bumped into Lorene.

"I'm sorry, dear," she said, her voice dripping with acid. "How clumsy of me."

Several seconds later, she and Lorene walked outside.

"Now," said Luke, "you go ahead, Congressman."

"I've said my piece—for now. You'll hear more from me once I get to San Francisco, where I can take proper action."

"Cornwallis, you do what you want. But don't threaten me. I gave a full report to Captain Freedley about what happened at Cottonwoods Station. He'll pass it along to the authorities and to John Butterfield. He's the only one who has any final say on this stage line."

"We'll see about that," Cornwallis grated. But Jenkins coughed loudly, and Cornwallis bit off anything else he was going to say. Luke watched the two men leave, his curiosity stirred by their odd behavior. There was more to it than simple animosity toward him. It was as if Jenkins and Cornwallis were using any excuse to attack Butterfield and the Overland Mail company stage line. It was something to think about.

As Lorene hurried to where the stagecoach was parked, her thoughts were a mixture of confusion and concern. She had seldom left her carpetbag out of her sight, but now she couldn't remember what she had done with it. It wasn't her personal effects that she was worried about—it was the sealed courier packet for her father from Senator Bell. She had taken such care with it—but now, in the aftermath of the events at Cottonwoods Station, she apparently had let her guard slip.

Lorene came around the coach to the open side door. Inside, Stuart Gorman was rattling something. She heard the rustle of cloth, the snick of paper, but she could not see him clearly in the darkened interior.

"Mr. Gorman?"

She heard a thunk as if something heavy had dropped to the floor.

"Huh?"

"What are you doing in there?"

"Nothing."

Lorene stepped up and saw her carpetbag on the floor. She didn't remember putting it there. Instead, she now recalled that she had placed it on the seat by the window while she washed up before breakfast. After washing she had started to retrieve it, but instead had been led to the mess hall by Anne Jenkins, that fluttery, nervous little woman.

"Were you going through my bag?" she asked Gorman.

"Uh, no, ma'am. I, uh, knocked it to the floor. Things, uh, spilled out and I was just putting everything back."

She picked up her bag and opened it. Everything was inside, but not where things were supposed to be. The packet from Senator Bell was there, as well. But on top—not in the bottom where she usually kept it.

"I—I'm awful sorry, Miss Martin."

She saw that he was genuinely upset and visibly contrite. She patted his hand and smiled at him. "That's all right. And please call me Lorene. No harm done."

"N-n-no," he stammered. "No harm done." He paused. "Miss, ah, Lorene . . . I—I uh . . ."

"Yes?" she asked.

And then Cornwallis's shadow filled the door.

"Nothing," said Stuart.

The rest of the passengers piled into the coach. Then Morty released the brake, snapped the whip, and the Concord rumbled through the open gate of the fort. The soldiers did not wave, and the passengers were too tense to even care about farewells.

A few miles later, the stage stopped briefly at Cookes Spring Station. There they were able to replace the four original horses, leaving them two fairly fresh cavalry horses to use as spares. Morty Tubbs learned from the stationmen that five riders trailing spare mounts had passed by without stopping just before dawn that morning. And two hours ago, an army lieutenant had stopped, asked questions, and ridden on after filling one of his canteens.

A few miles beyond Cookes Spring, Luke tapped Morty on the shoulder. "Hold up," he shouted. "Draw 'em in!"

Morty hauled in on the reins and set the brake. "What the hell, Luke . . . we ain't . . ." He stopped, following Luke's backward gaze.

The passengers rubbernecked out the side windows. "What's the trouble?" Jenkins called up.

"Lookee there!" shouted Morty.

A black column of smoke rose in the sky, rapidly billowing upward from a fire below it that could not be seen.

"Cookes Spring," said Luke.

"Apaches?" asked Tubbs, dumbstruck, a wad of tobacco wedged in his teeth.

"Better start 'em up again. We want to go through Cookes Pass in daylight."

As the stage rumbled forward, Luke eyed their back trail, the shotgun within easy reach. He knew that the men at Cookes Spring Station were probably dead, the station burning. For some reason, the Apaches were following them—letting them pass through, and blocking the way back. But why?

Again the question. And somewhere, beyond reach in his mind, there had to be an answer.

Chapter 5

Mimbres Station lay just ahead of the Yuma-bound coach. It would be the last stop before Cookes Pass. On the other side lay Cow Spring and Soldier's Farewell way stations. This was desolate country, and the miles wore down the driver and passengers. Morty was pushing hard, roiling up the dust, sending it spooling out behind him until it hung in the air like fog. Luke had dozed all morning, catching up on sleep he had missed, but now he jolted awake as he sensed a change in the team's rhythm.

"Ought to see the flag a-wavin' up there," yelled Morty, slowing the stage.

Luke's keen eyes swept the barren landscape. "Take her in slow," he told the driver as he leaned over the side and saw Jenkins's head poking out. "Keep your heads inside the coach," Luke ordered.

"I don't take orders from you, Faraday."

"Keep your head poked out then . . . that is, if you want an arrow or a tomahawk in your skull."

Jenkins jerked his head back inside the coach.

"Awful quiet," said Morty.

The team slowed to a walk. The horses started blowing. Their ears twitched, but none of them nickered or whinnied.

The station sprawled in the sun, the windows vacant, like eyeless sockets. Heat waves shimmered off the earth.

A turkey buzzard floated in the sky, spiraling on invisible currents, wings stretched to catch every wisp of air. A hawk floated low over the ground, its shadow racing to catch it. A quail *ca-ca-cawed* somewhere in a mesquite thicket.

Morty drew the team up and engaged the brake. Sweat gleamed in streaks on the horses' backs. Their tails swatted at flies. A Gila lizard lumbered out from under a shaded rock, its tongue flicking. Then it withdrew, slinking out of the boil of the sun.

Luke looked at every window. The door to the main building where meals were served was wide open. He looked at the corrals, the stables. The tack room was locked tight. He sniffed the air.

"Smells of Apache," he husked. "Not much, but a little."

"You can smell 'em?"

Luke climbed down, the double-barreled Greener shotgun nestled in both hands. He walked toward the station, a thumb laid across both hammers.

"Hallo!" he called.

No answer. It was as quiet as the noonday prairie.

He stepped inside the large adobe with its log rafters, gun ports, and sod roof. There was no one there. But it looked like whoever had been there had left in a mighty big hurry. Half-eaten food sat on a table near the big kitchen, the firebox was still hot and the coffeepot stood cold on a trivet.

There was a hastily scrawled note on the floor, which Luke picked up and read quickly: *Apaches took the horses last night. We gone south on foot, then east to El Paso— the only way. They all over. Might have got the eastbound and westbound coaches. Pray to God. Something's sure up.*

The note wasn't signed, but Luke knew that it had been written by a man they called Caleb Sour—a grumpy old man, but not easily scared. Until now.

Luke slipped the note inside his pouch, went to the door, and waved Morty in. The Apaches had come all right, and then had gone. Caleb had told them something in his note—not right out plain, but something he wanted anyone reading it to know.

Morty drove the team in and skidded them to a halt in a braking turn.

"Where's Caleb Sour?"

"Gone. Have the passengers grab some grub, and we'll get some bedrolls and tents from the station."

Morty swung down. "We goin' campin'?"

"Yeah, Morty, but not here. We'll make camp this side of the pass, so we can go through it at daybreak—just in case anyone's waiting."

"Might make the pass afore dark if we hurried."

"Yeah, but that's what they might be figuring."

Luke said no more then. Morty got the passengers disembarked and set the ladies to fixing lunch while he tended to the team. Meanwhile, Luke made a wide circle, checking for signs. What he found told him a great deal, but not what he wanted to know.

Morty walked out to meet Luke, and the two squatted down in the shade of a rock that jutted out of the ground at an angle providing an overhang. Luke showed the driver the note. Morty read it, with difficulty, then read it again. Luke picked up a sharp stone and drew small circles in the dirt.

"Seems to me Caleb Sour was plumb scairt," said Tubbs.

Faraday smoothed his mustache with a single sweep of his hand. "What's bothering me is that the Apaches seem so damned organized and sure of themselves. They were here, all right. All around the station. A few even came down into the yard. There are unshod hoofprints all over, like they made a big show. A man looking around would see Indians at every point of the compass."

"You're gettin' at somethin', Luke?"

"I am, but I'm not sure what yet. I've been thinking about old Caleb Sour. Apaches come in the night, slip into the corrals, and take the horses—that's pure Apache. Now that they've got the horses, why not just ride on back to their hideout and brag about how slick they were? But no—they come back at breakfast time and strut around, yelling, scaring the hell out of Caleb and his helpers. They even give them time to pack up and skedaddle. But Caleb doesn't go west through Cookes Pass over to Cow Spring. And he doesn't go east, back to Fort Fillmore where he'd have the army to protect him. Now that strikes me as right strange, until I saw what the Apaches had done to make Caleb go south.'' Luke pointed at one of the circles he had drawn in the dirt. ''Back to Fillmore would have been the easiest way if a man was running—it's all downhill.''

''That's the way I'da gone.''

Luke slashed a line across the circle. ''There's the road—the easy route—but the Apaches blocked it both ways. They let Caleb go out toward the south, and they told him in advance where he had to go. That's why his note said what it did: *the only way.* Caleb thinks the Apaches have the whole stage line under siege and have attacked the coaches in both directions. We're behind schedule, and the eastbound from Yuma hasn't shown anywhere along the line so far.''

''Mighty puzzlin'.''

''Yeah, Morty. The Apaches kill a soldier, burn out a station, run off men at another but let them live—as if they want word to get back to El Paso. And yet they don't attack our own stage. We're going through, just like it was planned.''

''You think they're going to let us go all the way to Yuma?''

Luke stood up, looked up toward the mountain range to the west, and drew in a breath. ''I don't know. Like Caleb Sour said, something's up. I don't know what, but I aim to find out. We'll camp off the trail tonight, but set guards. You sleep with one eye open.''

''You think one of the passengers is . . . ?''

''Don't say it, Morty. Not yet. Just step lightly, and don't forget about Bodine.''

Luke slapped Tubbs on the back as the stage driver rose from his squatting position. The two men walked down the slope to the station. Luke looked straight ahead, but Morty's head moved like an owl's, his eyes searching full circle for an Apache.

The sun was falling toward the mountain peaks to the west, and long shadows began to darken the stage road as the Yuma-bound coach approached the last stretch before Cookes Pass, which would take it across the Continental Divide.

Luke Faraday rode one of the army saddle horses ahead of the stage to scout a place to camp for the night. He chose solid ground—a box canyon. The stage could sit at the entrance, and they'd only have to defend themselves in one direction if they were attacked. The canyon was deep and long—not perfect, since the back wall was not sheer, but it would have to do. A lookout could walk a few yards to a hill and see the road, but the stage could not be seen.

Luke obliterated the stage tracks where they left the road by dragging brush over a wide area. An Apache would not be fooled for long, but it was better than leaving a clear sign. "This will be a cold night," Luke told the passengers. "No fires. You'll have to eat hardtack and jerky if you get hungry."

"Why are we stopping here?" asked Chastity.

"So we can go through Cookes Pass in daylight."

"You expect trouble?" Stuart asked.

"I never look for trouble, but we'll stand watches. You'll stand one same as the other men."

Stuart beamed. He glanced at Chastity to see if she had heard, but she was looking at Luke, disappointment clouding her face.

Cornwallis stood beside the stage, sipping from his flask as he fanned himself with a copy of *Harper's Weekly*. The Jenkins couple sat nearby on rocks cooled under the canyon wall. Lorene remained inside the coach, looking through her carpetbag.

Luke and Morty unhitched the team and, along with the two spare horses, took them deeper into the canyon. They hobbled the front legs of each horse to prevent them from straying, then brought back grain for them. Stuart carried a small barrel of water.

"Mind you don't give 'em much," said Morty. "Don't want 'em founderin', and they'll want it most come mornin'."

"Yes, sir," said Gorman, proud to be of help. But he was nervous, too, and jumped at every sound. Luke could not help thinking that he had something in his craw, and a young man should not have much to worry about. Gorman was green, but he didn't strike Luke as being a coward— just a little intimidated by his boss, Cornwallis. And that was something he'd have to outgrow in a hurry.

Back in the coach, Lorene looked at the courier packet carefully. She hefted it in her hand and stared at the official stamp. It was addressed to her father and was marked Extremely Confidential. She turned the packet over and saw that it was sealed tightly. Yet, something was not quite right.

She turned it back over and double-checked the handwriting. Senator Bell had addressed the envelope while she watched. But the script she stared at now was not his. Rather, it was careful forgery. She opened the packet. Instead of the papers she expected, there was only a copy of *Harper's*.

Luke took the twilight watch. This was the time of day when the light was tricky. Imagined shapes loomed up beyond the mouth of the box canyon. Noises were amplified and distorted. Only the mountains seemed unchanged as the land made the transition from the brilliance of day to the soft gentle landscape of dusk. The sun left a blaze across the sky that slowly faded from dazzling gold to rust, finally dimming to lavender. The molten glow, where it sank in the west beyond the mountains, held for a long time until even it was gone, leaving only an ashen sky and light that strained a man's eyes.

Lorene Martin waited until full dark before she left her tent. She and Chastity had separate tents under a projection of rocks, near the canyon entrance. Deeper in the canyon was the tent of Merle and Anne Jenkins. Against the north wall, Cornwallis had a larger tent to himself, with Stuart Gorman's tent pitched right next to it. Morty lay snoring in his bedroll outside on the flat ground. Luke had placed his bedroll near Morty, who had the next watch.

Lorene had watched through her tent flap a long time, until the light became swallowed by nightfall and Luke's tall shape disappeared in the deep shadows of the rocks and cacti.

She slid out of the tent, walking carefully over the stones, to the place where she had last seen him.

"Luke? . . . "

A shadow loomed beside her.

"You could have been shot. What are you doing out here?"

"I—I wanted to talk to you."

"Talk spoils the listening," he said somewhat gruffly.

"It's important." She drew close to him. He smelled of sweat and leather, dust and horseflesh. She breathed him in, heady from the nearness. Then, quickly, she told him of her trip to Washington and the packet she was carrying. "I saw Mr. Gorman going through my carpetbag," she finished.

Luke knew little of Cornwallis, and even less of Gorman. But he was a man used to making quick judgments and holding to them until something changed his mind. "Gorman doesn't strike me as the sneaky sort."

"I saw him. He was very upset."

"Could be he was doing it because he was ordered to. He works for Cornwallis, who probably knows Senator Bell's writing better'n anyone besides you."

"Yes," she sighed. "That's true. But I've been so careful. I'm sure no one has seen the packet."

"Apparently you're not the only one who knows of its existence," Luke commented.

"Can you help me get the packet back?" she asked.

"First you should talk to Gorman. First thing tomorrow, maybe. Just hit him straight out with it. Watch his face—his eyes."

"I—I'm so nervous I don't know if I can wait. The documents in that envelope are important to my father. I can't let him down."

"You wait till morning—nobody's going anywhere. You'll see his face plain then. Now go on back and get some sleep. Step careful—snakes do their hunting at night."

She cringed, but the feeling passed. Somehow, being with this man she was not afraid of anything. She felt his strength, his closeness. She turned to leave, then stopped and looked at him, trying to see his face. It was only a shadow, dimly perceived against the star-stippled sky.

"Luke?"

"Yes?"

"Are you—are you married?"

It seemed hours before he answered. "To a squaw woman. I got a Cheyenne wife, kids."

She tried to keep the disappointment out of her voice. "I—I see. Good night, Luke. Thanks for hearing me out."

"No trouble. You sleep tight, Lorene."

She felt a tingling inside her chest. The way he had said her name—there had been a gentleness in the sound. As she started away from him, she became aware that her heart was beating very fast. And her face felt hot against the coolness of the evening—burning as if bathed in steam.

Don't you dare, she told herself. *He's married. He said so. To a squaw! To a damned squaw!*

Stuart heard a rustling in Cornwallis's tent. Curious, he crawled to the flap of his own tent and peered out into the dark. The congressman stood a few feet away, a shadowy hulk. Then he walked away, carefully picking his steps, toward the tent where Merle and Anne Jenkins were sleeping.

Stuart was still dressed, unable to sleep. Cornwallis had made him do something that went against the grain: steal. And deceive. Those words flashed in young Stuart's brain as he thought about what he had done. He should have stood up to the man, but he hadn't been able to when Cornwallis had approached him.

"Young man," the congressman had said, "there are some bad people in this country who would force me out of public office—for their own gain. These people have prepared some trumped-up charges against me. Some reliable sources in Washington told me that woman, Miss Martin, is carrying certain false documents in her handbag that could be quite damaging. I want you to obtain those documents so that I can publicly expose these evildoers and safeguard the U.S. Constitution."

Cornwallis had been very persuasive. Certainly Stuart could understand how a man in such a high office would have enemies. And he had sworn loyalty to the congressman.

But now, Stuart wasn't so sure he had done the right thing. Deception was deception. Stealing was stealing.

And now where was Cornwallis going at this time of night? What business did he have with Jenkins? Stuart didn't like those two. Mrs. Jenkins was always watching him, whispering to her husband, passing notes to Cornwallis—keeping it all secret. He far preferred Lorene Martin. She didn't seem the kind of person who would be involved in a plot against the congressman. But she did have an official packet containing documents of some sort—it had been in her carpetbag just as the congressman had said. And she kept that carpetbag with her almost all the time, as if afraid to let it out of her sight. So, she had her secrets, too. But who was right?

There was no way to tell unless he knew what was contained in that packet he had turned over to the congressman. And maybe Lorene could tell him.

Stuart waited until he no longer heard Cornwallis

tiptoeing across the canyon. Quickly, he left his tent, closed the flap, and sneaked toward the women's tents. He knew which tent was hers. He bent down and opened the flap.

A hand gripped his shoulder from behind, fingernails dug into his flesh, and Gorman's blood froze. "God, don't shoot me," he breathed as he tried to turn and see who had caught him sneaking into the tent.

"Stuart! What are you doing?"

"Lorene? Miss Martin? I—I've got to talk to you."

"Yes, I expect you do. But not here. We'll wake Chastity." She led him away from the tents, pulling on his wrist.

He was shaking from dread. Lorene knew!

Some yards away, Lorene stopped. "You stole something from me," she accused. "I want it back!"

"I—he made me do it. The congressman. I had to take it."

"Where is it?"

"In his tent."

"How much did he pay you?"

He told her what the congressman had said about the packet, and finished by recounting how Cornwallis had left his tent a few moments before.

"He told you nonsense, Stuart. Wake up, I don't know what's in that packet, but it's not something anyone dreamed up." She told him of her father and how he had always thought that Cornwallis was cheating the public. Now, perhaps, he had proof. "You must get that packet back for me! Unless you're afraid to stand up to him. Anyone who would ask you to steal couldn't be a very trustworthy person, now could he?"

"No—no, I guess not."

"Hurry, get it while he's gone." She followed him to the congressman's tent and waited outside while he went in.

Stuart felt in the dark for the packet. His hand struck something hard, which tipped over and drenched his sleeve with liquid. As he grabbed the object and set it upright, he realized it was the flask of whiskey Cornwallis had been carrying this trip. But he noticed there was something odd about it—the smell. It didn't seem to have any. He held his sleeve close to his nose, licked the moisture, then lifted the flask and took a small swallow. It was little more than water. Quite strange. The congressman was making a big show of being tipsy, but it was obvious he hadn't gotten drunk drinking out of this bottle.

Stuart left the flask standing on the ground beside the congressman's bedroll and resumed his search. A short while later he found the courier packet, under the bedroll. The packet had been opened, but he could feel the papers were still inside. He went back outside and handed the packet to Lorene. His hand was shaking.

"It's been opened," she whispered. "Do you have a match? I must see what's in here."

"In my tent."

"Let's go!"

Inside, Stuart struck a match. Lorene glanced quickly at the papers, until the match went out. Stuart struck another, then another, as they both read the letter from Senator Bell to her father. In his missive, Bell explained that Cornwallis had agreed to resign from Congress to avoid being censured and impeached. He wrote that the enclosed documents contained evidence proving Cornwallis illegally feathered his own nest during the money panic in 1857, sold political favors to special San Francisco interests, and was involved in a land scheme in southern California at El Rancho San Bernardino.

But the most startling part of the letter concerned his present scheme:

"Here, too, is the documented evidence," it read, "that connects Cornwallis with a plot having far-reaching consequences. You will see that he is deeply involved with Mr. Jeffries, whose own stage line has suffered since Congress approved John Butterfield's route. Jeffries wants the overland mail contract and will stop at nothing to discredit Butterfield, including bribery and violence."

Lorene gasped. Now her own hands were shaking.

She stuffed the documents back in the envelope. "Not a word about this," she said. "If what Senator Bell says is true, then we have to let someone in authority know about this right away."

"But who? We're miles from any authority."

"I know someone. Trust me."

Lorene left Stuart and returned to her own tent. She crawled inside, closed the flap, and put the packet under her pillow. She fell asleep thinking of Luke Faraday and hoping he was the man she believed him to be—the only one who could help her expose Cornwallis before he accomplished his evil task.

Luke heard the sound—faint, elusive. The tink of stone on stone.

He held his breath, listening. Was it only his imagination? A rabbit? A coyote slinking past?

For a long time there was nothing. Then, the scrape of a boot on grit. Someone was moving around out there, beyond the canyon entrance, off where no one should be. Luke's turn on watch was almost over, and he had made a wide loop toward the road, just to assure himself that it was safe to wake up Morty for the next shift. Now it appeared someone was up to something near their camp. A sleepwalker? Or . . . ?

Faraday hefted the Hawken rifle, crouching low. He moved slowly, listening between each step. Step, stop, wait, listen.

A rock rattled, dislodged by a boot. A heavy object brushed over sand. The shapes around him rose up out of the shadows, and he almost stepped into a beaver-tail cactus before he realized what it was. The ocotillos seemed to move, beckoning with long outstretched arms.

A yucca rattled as someone or something brushed against it. A twig snapped, sounding almost like a distant rifle shot.

Luke moved faster, toward the sound. His boots dropped lightly on soft sand. He knew the ways of hunting—game or men—but this was a time of shadows and false sounds, stalking through a dream landscape of deceptive silhouettes, where every shape could be deadly.

He stopped again, moving his head in a half circle to pick up any sound.

Ahead, faintly lit by starlight, a shadow moved from behind a tall boulder. Luke stepped forward, hunching low. The shadow turned and came toward him.

And then Luke made a mistake. He knew it even as he was in the act. He stopped, raised the Hawken, and cocked it back. And the hammer click reverberated through the canyon.

From somewhere behind him, off to the side, he heard the *whisk-whisk* of something arcing through the air. He opened his mouth to challenge the figure behind him, then tried to twist away, but even as he braced himself for the blow, he knew it was too late.

Blinding, dazzling lights exploded in Luke's skull.

He pitched forward, falling into space. He did not feel the earth as he hit it. His mind pooled with darkness, and the blazing lights danced away, leaving only a great silence and a vast empty dark.

"Get him, Hiram?"

"I—I got him, Merle." Cornwallis was panting, trembling with excitement and accomplishment. "Give me a minute."

Merle walked back to the crates and sat down. They had worked for over an hour getting them this far without being discovered. The hardest part had been unlashing them from the stage and handing them down.

Cornwallis began breathing steadily. He walked over to Merle. "Don't know how long he'll stay down. We've got a lot to do."

The two crates were stacked. Merle took the front end, Cornwallis the rear. They puffed and panted toward the road. When it was in sight, a faint tawny ribbon visible only because of the absence of cactus, they reconnoitered.

Jenkins walked down the road back toward El Paso. In a few minutes he was back. "I found a good spot."

They carried the crates to a small washout near a clump of beaver-tail cactus. They set the crates in the depression, then began scooping sand to cover them. Merle found a stone and positioned it as a marker on top of the sand covering the crates.

"Now," said Jenkins, "we set stones on the road like he told me."

They found small stones and placed them in an arrow pattern on the edge of the road. The tip of the arrow pointed to the cache.

"Do you think Mangas Sangrías will find them?" asked Cornwallis, his voice a harsh whisper.

"He'll find them. He's right behind us. May have a brave watching us right now."

Hiram's scalp prickled. "Let's get out of here," he said. "If we're caught with those rifles, this trip'll be one way—to the Yuma hangman."

"Just wait," said Merle, "until Mangas gets his hands on those newfangled Spencer repeating rifles. The army doesn't even have them yet. He'll have the cavalry tucking tail and running all along the stage route."

Cornwallis nervously nodded. The Apaches would have had the upper hand with Spencers if he had not substituted cheaper, single-shot rifles for them, pocketing the difference. With the Spencers, the Apaches could have forced Butterfield to relinquish his contract for the stage line. That was why Merle had offered Mangas the newly invented repeaters and had made Cornwallis promise to obtain two sample crates with which to seal their deal. And that was why Cornwallis was now so very uneasy. For he alone knew what those crates really contained—and he shuddered to think what Mangas's reaction would be upon receiving them. When Hiram had departed Washington with the crates, he had thought the journey to be a lark and the Indians an inferior ally who would do what they were told and be thankful for whatever they got. But now, after seeing the death of Ned Cooper and the burning of Cookes Spring Station, he was no longer so sure.

Well, they're not repeaters, but at least they're rifles,

he consoled himself. And anyway, there was nothing he could do to change things now. There was no turning back. Sick as he was inside over the way things were turning out, Cornwallis could only continue with his deceptions—not only for the sake of others, but for himself as well.

Chapter 6

Morty shook Luke Faraday awake. Dawn was a pale light slipping over the land like a wide river going over its banks.

"You fall asleep on the job, Luke?"

Faraday rose up, groggy with a dull pain at the back of his head. He wiped grit from his mouth and blew sand from his nostrils. His clothes were slick with dew, and his joints felt as if they had been worked over with a knotted lariat. Bones creaked, muscles strained as he sat up and lifted his rifle from the ground. He checked the muzzle and wiped a thin patina of sand from around the bore. No dirt had gotten inside, apparently.

"I lost a night somewhere," Luke said sheepishly as he came slowly to his feet.

"Well, you lost more'n that."

"Huh?"

"Somebody's been up on that stage. I found some loose bindings and a couple of crates missing. Think they was them awnings."

"Awnings?"

"That's what the crates said. But don't pay no nevermind. We got to get movin'. I been scoutin' for you nigh on to half an hour. Thought you was done in fer sure."

"Anybody up besides you?"

Tubbs shook his head and spat a stream of tobacco juice into the air. It splatted on a prickly pear, dripping down its scarred trunk.

"Well, I got my bearings. I can track whoever skulled me."

"Dammit, we ain't got time fer that. You want to get through that pass early, we got to hitch up, move on out."

Luke considered it. He wanted to know who had knocked him cold, but he did have the passengers to think about.

"We better wake 'em up," Morty said, nodding toward the camp. "You want to take on that chore?"

"Sure, and I'll help you hitch the team when I finish."

Luke woke up the Jenkins couple first. Merle was fully dressed, his clothes wrinkled.

"You have a good night?" Luke asked, eyeing Merle suspiciously.

"Thought I was supposed to stand a watch."

"You got lucky."

Anne Jenkins glared at Faraday, then gathered her things and walked off toward the back of the canyon to complete her toilet. Merle watched as Luke awakened Cornwallis and Gorman.

Cornwallis frowned when he emerged from his tent. "Sleep tight?" Luke asked, watching the congressman's eyes very carefully.

"I've slept better. At least it was quiet."

"Was it? You didn't hear anyone prowling around?"

"I assure you, sir, that I heard nothing extraordinary. Was someone . . . ?" But Faraday already had walked away.

As Stuart Gorman stepped groggily from his tent, Cornwallis looked sharply at his young aide. "You let me down, Stuart. I won't forget it."

"I—I . . ."

"Did you let that woman persuade you to steal back the documents?"

"I should never have done what you asked, sir. It was wrong."

"You wouldn't know what was wrong, you young whelp!"

Stuart flinched when he saw the look in the congressman's eyes. But he already felt better about getting the packet back to Lorene. He wished he had the courage to tell Cornwallis what he felt. He wished he could resign on the spot. But that murderous look in the older man's eyes made him bite his lip and hold back. This was not the time.

Lorene Martin and Chastity Blaine were already stepping from their tents as Faraday approached.

"Good morning, ladies," he smiled. "We'll be pulling out just as soon as we can get these tents packed."

"We must have breakfast first," insisted Chastity. "A good warm meal before we continue on our journey."

"That will have to wait until lunch," Luke replied. "We don't want any smoke."

"But the coach will throw up dust. What's the difference?"

"Young lady, you have a very sharp tongue and you're probably right, but every moment of delay lessens our chance of getting through that pass."

Lorene stepped closer to Luke. She was no longer wearing a dress, but had put on riding breeches, boots, and a blouse that looked as if it had been fitted just for her. The clothes fit tightly, and Luke's eyes seemed to smoke when he looked at her.

"Are you expecting someone to be in that pass?" she asked.

"Maybe."

"Bodine?"

"Yes. Or the Apaches."

"Then I'd like to ride one of the spare horses, carry a rifle and pistol."

"You'll ride in the coach like the others, miss. You're a paying passenger, not an armed guard."

Lorene's cheeks flamed. Her green eyes flashed her annoyance. She wanted to say more, but Faraday had turned on his heel and walked toward the coach.

"Ooooh, that man!" she exclaimed.

"He's rather mean, isn't he?" said Chastity, with a hint of a smile. "And crude."

Lorene stamped her heel and clenched her fists until the knuckles turned white. "He's terrible," she said. "He—he makes me feel like a little girl at times."

"But you like him, don't you?" blurted Chastity, immediately regretting her words. "I mean . . ."

"I know what you mean," snapped Lorene. "Come on, let's get packed. We don't want to keep *Mr.* Faraday waiting."

When the horses were hitched, Stuart Gorman approached Faraday.

"I—I'd like to ride with you and Mr. Tubbs," he said quietly. "I don't want to be in the coach with Mr. Cornwallis." He stared downward sheepishly.

Luke saw that the young man was earnest—under pressure of some sort. "You ride up with us, son," he said.

Stuart's grin broke wide, and he seemed to grow a good half foot. "Thanks, Mr. Faraday."

"Call me Luke. I don't guarantee the ride'll be any fun. You'll pack a loaded rifle and keep your eyes peeled sharp. And if I were you I'd wear a hat. That sun'll drive you plumb loco sitting up high in the open like that."

Lieutenant Stack headed into Cookes Pass just after dawn. He, too, had camped east of the pass—not far from the stage. He knew from past experience that the two-mile stretch ahead could conceal a lot of trouble. He was weary, stiff from sleeping on lumpy ground. Now, as he rode slowly up into the pass, he was alert, his senses keen. If there was going to be a place where Bodine set a trap for his pursuers, this would be it. Either here or at Apache Pass farther to the west, but the tracks he was following were only a day old. And they were Bodine's tracks, he knew for certain.

Ernie Bodine saw Stack from his position halfway through the pass. The sun was at the lieutenant's back, so

that at first the outlaw couldn't determine who the lone
rider was.

Will Peeker edged forward over the rock, and Bodine
hissed him down. Peeker glared at Bodine. This was their
second day of waiting, and no one liked it much. They had
grub, but it was tasteless. Their beards were getting scratchy.
Their clothes reeked with the sour smell of sweat. And the
sun was hell, pure hell. Long days of endless monotony
were beginning to grate at the men—jerk at their nerves
like cactus thorns.

Bodine didn't know if he could keep them together
much longer. Peeker was beginning to be a problem—like
a small sharp stone inside a boot. Jim Culhane was getting
edgy, and Dan Rawlings had gone silent, which wasn't a
good sign, but at least he didn't mutter under his breath
like Will and Jim. Rafe Adams was getting flint eyed and
spooky, maybe because he wanted to grab the payroll
money and get out of this furnace, which sucked at their
skin and dried out their throats, filling their lungs with
stale, dead air. But this was where the stagecoach had to
pass, and that Blaine gal was mighty important. Chastity
could be the ticket to get Chet Morgan out of Yuma. And
Bodine wanted Morgan's share of the army payroll.

So did Rafe Adams. Rafe, sensing a change in Bodine,
climbed out from under a rock where he had crawled like a
lizard to seek shade. "You see the stage, Ernie?"

"Just a soldier, Rafe. Pickin' his way. Follerin' tracks
like a goddamned coonhound."

Rafe slid in beside Bodine and peered over the rock.
Heat waves shimmered off the trail, blurring the image of
the man in blue on a chestnut horse. Rafe's eyes narrowed,
trying to shut out the dancing land that shook his senses
and blurred his vision. There was something about the
rider that was familiar.

Jim Culhane licked his parched, cracked lips and tried
to focus his eyes on the small figure of the approaching
rider. He cursed and looked up the line at Will Peeker,
trying to make eye contact. Peeker had slid back from

sight, sweat pouring down the stock of his rifle where his hands gripped its wood.

Dan Rawlings, wedged between two boulders, kept smearing dirt on his rifle barrel to keep the sun from glinting off the metal. The bluing on his .50-caliber rifle was faded, and the outer metal was pitted after years of use. He, too, saw the rider—a speck at the far end of the pass, riding steady, looking at tracks.

"You want him?" Rafe asked Bodine.

"Maybe. Maybe not. He could be by hisself or trackin' fer a posse."

"That looks like the lieutenant who brought you to the stage in El Paso."

"I know, Rafe," Bodine snapped.

"Easy, Bodine. In another ten minutes he'll be in range. He might spook before that."

"Hell, you talk like a desk soldier, Rafe."

"I put in my time."

Bodine looked at Rafe with sun-glazed eyes. "Yeah, you did at that." He remembered the campaign at Victor in California, when they chased the Serrano Indians to Chimney Rock, put them down with cannons, and then charged in on horses to finish them off. It stretched the truth to call it a campaign—it really had been a massacre, with the Indians never having a chance—but Rafe had been in on it.

Down in the pass, Stack rode on, kicking his horse into a rocking canter.

Bodine grinned. They had played it right when they rode straight on through Cookes Pass and then doubled back into the rocks above the pass, where they had tied their horses and the spare army mounts and then had taken positions overlooking the stage road. The bluecoat was going for it—lock, stock, and barrel.

Stack thought now that Bodine and his bunch must have ridden through the pass and kept on going. The tracks showed that—horses running without stopping, picking up speed on the flat.

The lieutenant dug in his spurs. His mount hesitated,

then started to pick up the gait. That's when Stack saw the flash of sun glinting off metal.

He reined in hard and reached for his rifle. He saw the puff of smoke before he heard the report—a distant crack, the sound a rifle makes.

Something tugged at his shoulder. A second later, searing pain shot through the muscle. A sticky wetness soaked his shirt at the shoulder and a wave of dizziness swept over him. The sky spun dizzily, the rocks where the shot had come from all blurred together in daubs and smears of color. Reflexively, his left arm tightened down on the reins, the bit pulling at the horse's mouth. Stack felt himself still going forward as the horse slid to a stop. He pitched forward, and the ground rushed up to meet him.

Stack threw up an arm to ward off the impact and felt a wrench as his leg caught in the stirrup, pulling him up short. His elbow scraped rock, but the pain was far away, too dull to matter. His shoulder was a firebrand raging out of control.

Blood rushed to his brain as he hung there, one foot in the stirrup, his horse holding steady. A cloud of blackness billowed in his brain, and he lost consciousness. Blood dripped from his shoulder into the dust, forming little craters, then a series of interconnecting rivulets that joined together in a muddy pool.

"Nice shot, Bodine," said Rafe Adams.

"Off. Low, and about six inches wide. I was aiming for his damned head."

"Want me to go down and finish him off?" Peeker asked. "I'm gettin' cramped sittin' here doin' nothin'."

"Hell, looka there," said Bodine. "Here comes the stage. You better sit tight."

"Think they heard the shot?" Rafe asked.

"I doubt it—too far away. Might have seen the gun smoke, though."

"What about him?" Adams asked, pointing at Stack. The lieutenant's head was crooked at a crazy angle, his leg twisted where the horse had turned slightly.

"Leave him. He's going to set it up for us, Rafe.

They'll have to stop now. And when they do, we'll take 'em and get the Blaine girl. Easy as puddin'.''

Rafe looked at his partner and shuddered. Bodine was grinning, an insane light dancing in his eyes. Bodine had changed a lot since they'd planned the payroll robbery. Maybe it was from having cheated the hangman—or from the blood on his hands. Or maybe Yuma Prison had stirred up something terrible inside him that had been there all the time—waiting.

"You hear anything?" Luke shouted to Morty. The stage rumbled up the grade, pulling more slowly.

"I heard it," said Stuart Gorman. "A rifle."

"You boys done had your brains bounced too much coming up this grade. I didn't hear nothin' but horses breakin' wind and leather creakin'.''

"Haul 'em up, Morty."

Morty started to protest. Then he saw the look on Luke's face—dead serious as he stared up into the pass. Morty stopped the team. Voices hummed from inside the coach.

"I'm going to saddle up and ride on ahead," Luke said. "Won't hurt any to scout. You make sure everyone stays close, and check the rifles and pistols. This may be the time we'll have to use them."

Luke saddled quickly, as Cornwallis helped the women out of the coach.

"We'll stretch our legs," Cornwallis snorted. "If we keep stopping like this, it'll take a year to get to San Francisco."

Faraday rode off. He thought he had seen something, but couldn't be sure. It wasn't much—a dark shape, something moving in the rocks. A few minutes later, he saw Stack's horse and the lieutenant hanging lifelessly from the stirrup. Luke's eyes scanned the rocks and the brush. Someone could be up there, but why hadn't they gotten Stack out of the way?

The lieutenant's horse, seeing Faraday, perked its ears and nickered. It took a few paces forward, and Stack's foot came loose, his leg coming down with a jarring thud. The lieutenant, as if jolted back to consciousness, rolled over and struggled to rise.

"Damn! He's alive!" Luke muttered to himself. Maybe Stack had been in a running fight and got shot as the outlaws rode off, Luke thought. Or he could be bait.

"Help me!" moaned Stack. "Faraday? Is that you?"

Stack tried to stand and his leg went out from under him. He screamed in pain as he came down on his wounded shoulder.

Luke jerked his Hawken from the rifle scabbard and slid out of the saddle. Cautiously, he approached the wounded soldier.

"That's Faraday," muttered Bodine. "The sonofabitch that caught me in the Huecos."

"It's him, all right," said Adams. "You gonna shoot him?"

"He's with that stage. If we shoot him, it'll turn and run. Peeker, you think you can sneak around and take him from behind while he's goin' after the soldier? Use a knife. He can't be seen from the stage, so they'll come on."

"I can do it," said Culhane. "Peeker's no good with a knife."

"Suit yourself," said Bodine. "We'll wait till the stage hits the pass, then ride on down and take 'em."

"What'll we do with the spare horses?" Rafe asked, thumbing back toward where they had tied their mounts with the spare army horses they had taken at Cottonwoods Station.

"No problem," Bodine grinned. "This job'll be smooth as butter, and then we'll jes' light back up here and pick 'em up." He turned back to Culhane. "Now get to it!"

Luke knew he was taking a risk, but he couldn't leave Stack out there in the open like that. And Stack wouldn't stand a chance if someone didn't tie off his wound. As Luke approached, he could see that the man had already lost considerable blood, and from the looks of him, he was still bleeding. As Faraday bent down to lift him up and carry him off the exposed roadway, Luke's eyes flicked to the rocks above, searching for a sign of any ambushers.

"Don't move till I tell you," Stack whispered to the bounty hunter. "You got a man sneaking up on you." Stack's whisper was so low that Luke could hardly hear him. But he froze, pretending to be looking at Stack's shoulder.

"You hurt bad?"

"Not as bad as they think. Bodine's up there, and I saw a man drop out of the brush just as you came up."

The short hairs on Luke's neck prickled. "Tell me where he is, Stack."

"Right now he's just about in range . . ."

"What?"

"Duck, Faraday!"

Luke threw himself forward as Stack rolled away, jerking his pistol up in a single smooth motion. Luke saw that he'd had it ready all the time. As he twisted, he saw a man lunge, knife blade flashing in the sun.

Stack cocked and fired. The ball struck the attacker square in the chest, throwing him back off his feet, dead before he hit the rocks behind him.

Luke rolled again, cocking the Hawken. Suddenly, explosions shattered the air as puffs of white smoke blossomed on the hillside above the road—deadly blossoms. Stack scrambled toward the cover of brush, firing his Remington .44 revolver. Luke fired below a pall of smoke and ran toward Stack. He didn't stop, but reached down and grabbed the lieutenant's good arm, dragging him to cover behind some rocks.

Pistol fire rattled from above them, and lead balls smacked off stone or whined through the mesquite like angered hornets.

"We're pinned down!" gasped the wounded lieutenant.

"Just keep your head down and let them use up their rounds. When they go to reload, we'll back off. I've got a pistol, and I'll have this Hawken loaded in another minute."

"You alone, Faraday?"

"Damned if I know, Stack. It's beginning to look that way."

Morty Tubbs heard the gunfire drift around the bend in the road—a single shot, followed by a short volley. He yelled at the passengers to get back in the stage.

"Are you taking us out of danger?" demanded Cornwallis.

"Hell no! If Luke's in trouble, he'll need all the guns he can get. Now climb in that stage, Congressman, or I'll just leave you to die of thirst! I'm goin' ahead, and I ain't turnin' back for no yellowbelly, whatever his danged title is!"

"Your insolence, sir, is intolerable!"

"Them four-bit words ain't gonna keep this stage from rollin'!"

The crackle of pistol fire continued as Morty began unwrapping the reins from the brake. Lorene Martin threw her carpetbag up beside the driver, grasped a handhold, and pulled herself up onto the seat.

As Morty released the brake, Merle and Anne Jenkins scrambled into the coach, followed by a grumbling Cornwallis, his face livid under flaring whiskers.

Some distance away, Stuart and Chastity watched in horror as the coach started to roll. They started running after Morty, waving and yelling, but their shouts were lost in the rumble of wheels and the pounding of hooves.

Lorene grabbed the shotgun and laid it across her lap.

"You know how to use that, miss?" Morty cracked.

"Just bring me within range of whoever's shooting at Luke—at Mr. Faraday."

Morty grinned and spat tobacco from a corner of his mouth. "We'll do 'er!" he cackled, rattling the reins. As the coach lurched ahead, Morty half stood, urging the team to greater speed. He sat down when they hit their stride. He pulled his revolver from his holster and slid the barrel under his leg.

Lorene's copper-gold hair flew in the wind as the stage careened around the bend. There, ahead of them,

Luke and Stack stood up, firing above them. There was no return fire.

Morty jerked both hands backward, clamping fingers on the reins. He raised a boot, kicked on the brake, and as the coach skidded sideways, he fought to bring it under control. Lorene ducked to avoid an overhanging branch.

"Whoa, whoa!" Morty shouted, the brake screeching on the wheel.

Luke shoved Stack toward the stage, then stopped short. Around the bend, Chastity and Stuart ran into view. Above them, horses appeared on the skyline.

"Take cover!" shouted Luke. He started running toward them, waving his free arm.

Bodine, Rafe, and Peeker swooped down onto the road, pistols blazing. Balls sizzled close to Morty and Lorene atop the stage. No shots came from inside the coach as the passengers hit the floor, hugging it in fear.

Chastity hiked her skirts and ran faster. Unable to see the horsemen, she and Stuart ran only for the safety of the coach. Bullets kicked up spurts of dust around them.

Rafe kicked his horse and swung it wide. Behind him, Bodine and Peeker bore down on Stack and Faraday. Bodine hunched over, sighted down the pistol barrel, and squeezed. A ball struck Faraday in the thigh, smacking into flesh with a sound like a cork popping from a bottle. Luke's leg went out from under him, and he pitched forward, his Hawken rattling as it struck a rock.

"Get the gal!" shouted Bodine.

Lorene swung on him, but Morty was in the way, blocking her shot. Morty fired at Peeker but missed—and the stage team panicked in their traces, twisting and churning, threatening to tangle the lines. Morty struggled to settle them down as Peeker rode past. Stack, out of ammunition, leaned against the coach, gasping for breath, his wound throbbing with the drum of a dozen hammers.

Rafe Adams charged straight toward Chastity Blaine.

Gorman shouted at her, his words buried under the sound of pounding hooves.

Chastity saw the horseman bearing down on her, and

she shrieked and changed direction, twisting her ankle. She went down and got back up, limping slightly as she tried to avoid Adams.

"Stop!" shouted Stuart, racing toward Adams. "Leave her alone!"

Rafe leaned over the side of his horse, raising his arm. As Stuart rushed between him and Chastity, he swung the barrel of his pistol. It struck Gorman in the head, staggering him. He tumbled head over heels as the horse's shoulder brushed against him.

Chastity stopped short, screaming. Rafe holstered his pistol and reached out for the terrified girl, who stood immobilized, her head twisting to find a path of escape. Rafe's arm encircled her waist. Her feet left the ground as he snatched her up and threw her across the saddle in front of him. Then he drew his pistol again and wheeled the horse, shouting "I got her, Ernie!"

Bodine drew up and turned his horse. Peeker followed suit. Rafe passed them both, his horse's hooves flying. He held the pistol to Chastity's head.

Lorene saw Rafe coming and raised her shotgun to shoot him out of the saddle. Morty watched her in horror, then knocked the Greener down. "You might kill the gal!" he yelled.

Lorene's face drained to chalk.

Luke hobbled toward the stagecoach, his pistol empty and useless, as Bodine and Peeker rode by in a cloud of choking dust. Rawlings held up, his pistol jammed.

"They're getting away!" Lorene screamed.

Morty drew a bead on Bodine's back and squeezed the trigger. The hammer thunked dully against an empty cylinder.

The sound of hoofbeats faded, and the dust settled lazily back to the ground. Stuart Gorman staggered up, holding his swollen head. An egg-sized knot jutted from his scalp.

"You hurt bad, Luke?" Morty called down from the stage in the ensuing silence.

"I'll make it. The ball tore a hunk out of me, is all."

Luke ripped out a bandanna and tied a hasty tourni-
quet above the wound. A thumb-sized hole attested to the
bullet's passage through the meaty part of his thigh.

"They got Chastity!" Gorman blurted. He was on the
edge of hysteria.

"Calm down, son. I'm going after them," Luke said.

Lorene, still seated on the driver's seat, opened her
carpetbag and withdrew a loaded pistol and holster. The
Colt pocket pistol, .31 caliber, looked small, its brass
frame gleaming in the sun. She also removed the courier
packet and stuffed it into her waistband. "I'm going with
you," she said calmly. "You can't do it alone."

Cornwallis and the Jenkinses dropped meekly out of
the coach. Anne quickly began to examine the wounded
lieutenant, who had sat down on the stage's running board.

"She's right, you know," Stack said wearily, winc-
ing as Mrs. Jenkins touched his shoulder. "You can't do it
alone, Faraday."

"Looks like you got no choice, Luke," said Morty.

"You lost some blood, and those boys'll have a field day
if you ride up on 'em wounded."

"Saddle a horse, then," Luke told Lorene. "And
pack a bedroll and grub. Some of you others help the
lieutenant into the stage, then get that thing out of the
road." He pointed toward the body of Jim Culhane.

Lorene concealed a smile of satisfaction as she drew
in a deep breath and hopped down from the driver's seat.

"Watch my bag for me, Mr. Tubbs," she said jauntily.

"I'll do that, lady," he grinned, tobacco juice seep-
ing out of the corners of his mouth. "You take care."

Chapter 7

Two hours after riding out of Cookes Pass, Bodine waved his men to an abrupt halt. Rafe Adams cursed his partner under his breath for having left the spare horses tied in the rocks above the pass. There had been no chance to retrieve them, and now Rafe's horse was close to foundering under the weight of its double load.

Chastity Blaine, holding tight to the horn of Rafe's saddle, blinked into the desert sunlight and focused on the object blocking the road ahead: the burned-out hulk of a stagecoach. The coach seemed to hang upon a jumble of rocks, tilting on a broken front axle. Bullet holes pocked the leather. The charred wood glistened in the sun like a crow's wing. Arrows jutted from the wooden frame. The driver lay slumped on the seat, his teeth bared in the hideous fixation of death. The shotgun rider lay on his stomach under a wheel. The passengers had tried to run and had been shot down without mercy. Clothes and baggage lay strewn in all directions. The traces were cut and the horses were gone.

Chastity recoiled in horror when she saw a Gila monster hiss and crawl under an elderly woman's stiffened arm.

"Apaches," Rafe said.

"Makes your skin crawl, don't it?" said Bodine. "Explains what happened to the eastbound from Yuma."

86

"I don't like it none," said Peeker. "Them savages sure as hell got somethin' stuck in their craw."

Chastity held her hand over her mouth. Bile rose in her throat. She sat in front of Rafe on his horse, her leg muscles aching, her face pale.

"Drink some water, girl, you'll feel better," said Adams, slipping a canteen from his saddle horn.

"N-no. I—I can't. Do we have to stay here?"

"Cow Spring's just up the road," said Peeker. "Reckon the station got hit by the same bunch?"

"Apaches on the rampage are pure hell," said Bodine. "Let's ride."

Chastity held tight to the saddle horn as the horses moved away from the teetering coach and the buzzards floated in from perches concealed among the rocks and cacti, darkening the ground with their gaunt, ungainly bodies.

Dan Rawlings lingered, looking closely at the arrows. Finally, he rode up to the coach, leaned over, and broke off a shaft. He looked carefully at the fletching and the markings. Then he clapped spurs to his horse's flanks and caught up with Bodine.

He held out the broken arrow. Bodine looked at it and shrugged.

"Might be we oughta ride right on by Cow Spring," Dan drawled.

"How so?"

"This here's an Apache arrow, all right. But no laze-around-the-fort Injun shot it. This here's Mangas's bunch."

"An Injun's an Injun."

"This Bleeding Sleeves ain't no Apache to fool with. He's a Mimbreño, and plenty mean. He'd have to be on the warpath serious to tangle with the U.S. mails."

Rafe listened to the talk, watching Bodine as he rode along. Chastity's cheeks were beginning to regain their color, but the talk only brought back the memory of what they had seen back there on the road. The sickness boiled her insides again, and she fought to keep from retching.

"He's right, Ernie," Rafe agreed. "If Mangas is on the warpath, we'd best ride wide of the next station."

"We scoot clear of Cow Spring, then?" asked Bodine.

"Might be some safer," said Adams.

"Then you ride ahead, Rawlings," said Bodine, "and set us a line for Apache Pass. Can you keep us from gettin' lost?"

"I know the country," said Rawlings, spurring his horse. "It'll be rough going and a long way 'tween drinks."

As soon as he was gone, Bodine turned to his partner. "Where'd you get him, Rafe? He thinks he knows everything about Injuns."

"He scouted for a while, killed a trooper in a card game, and hit the trail. He'll do."

"Trash," said Bodine. "And Peeker, too."

Peeker heard Bodine and dropped back, his eyes drawn to murderous slits. But he had heard Rawlings, too, and knew that if Mangas was anywhere around, they might never reach the payroll cache. But if they did, he had a payoff of his own for Bodine. There was Johncock to think about—and Jim Culhane. And there was the girl riding with Adams. Out here a man thirsted for more than water.

Back in Cookes Pass, it was taking Luke and Lorene far longer than he would have liked to set out on the trail of Bodine. But it wasn't the woman who was holding things up. It was Faraday's thigh wound.

Luke poured a quarter pint of Morty's whiskey on the wound. The raw flesh sizzled and flared. Blood oozed up into the exposed flesh, but did not run free. He smeared some healing unguent on the wound, wrapped it loosely with a strip of cloth, and pulled fresh trousers on over the makeshift bandage. He stood out of sight behind a low hill, hoping Lorene had her horse saddled and their provisions packed.

Lorene pulled the cinch tight, testing it under the horse's belly with four fingers. Tight enough. Then she stuffed the courier packet into the saddlebag. Morty, cutting a fresh plug of tobacco while leaning against a rock, watched her work.

"Morty," she said, her voice just above a whisper, "will—will Bodine hurt Chastity? I mean . . ."

"I know what you're drivin' at, miss. But I don't rightly know about Bodine or them others. You keep at their heels, they might not do much."

"I know Mr. Faraday doesn't want me along. His wife must have a terrible life with him. When does he ever see her?"

Morty bit down on the chunk of tobacco, looking at her with a puzzled expression on his face.

"His wife?"

"Yes. He told me about the squaw he married and all his children. . . ."

"Haw, haw!" Tubbs guffawed. "He told you 'bout that Injun squaw he married? And all them little papooses?"

Lorene's face flushed a deep pink. She squinched her lips together in a scowl, her green eyes flashing with sudden anger. "I don't see what's funny about it."

Morty slapped his leg and danced an impromptu jig, hopping about in a circle. Anne Jenkins peered at him from inside the coach, an exasperated look shadowing her face.

Lorene grabbed her horse's reins and jerked them involuntarily.

"Now, now, miss, don't get yourself all heated up." Morty stopped laughing, but his eyes were wet with merriment and his mouth was drawn up in a bow. "I wasn't laughin' at you, necessarily, but you done bit the hook and swallowed the worm."

"What do you mean?"

"Hell, Luke ain't married to nobody. He must like you an awful lot fer him to feed you that yarn."

"I—I don't understand."

"Course you don't! Faraday's gun-shy, that's all. Woman gets too close to him, he tells her right off he's hitched to a squaw. And if he told you 'bout a passel of kids, it means he's mighty scairt of you. Yep, Luke's stayed away from the preacher fer a long spell by usin' that squaw tale, and you must be mighty special fer him to lay on all the beadwork like that. Yes sirree, ol' Luke's runnin' scairt with his tail tucked 'tween his legs!''

"Are you saying that he's not married?''

"Nope. Not to no squaw ner to any white gal. You watch him, miss, 'cause he's likely to go howlin' at the moon one of these nights. The man's in love fer true, and if you want him, you go after him. Wouldn't be a bad match, no sir, 'cause he's honest and hardworking. And, 'twixt you and me, I think he's ready to give up this bounty huntin' and settle down somewheres. But don't you tell him I told you this, or he'll skin me alive!''

Lorene pursed her lips and cocked her head. "He lied to me, Morty, and I can't forgive him for that. I felt sorry for him at first, and then for his wife. But if he doesn't have a wife, then I guess I feel cheated.''

"He never had no wife at all, and that's 'cause of what happened to his own sisters. Both of 'em older'n him and married, and both mean as sin. They drove their menfolk to drink and disaster, and Luke said he didn't want no part of womanhood. His own pa, too, was drove off by a shrew wife who bled him, marrowed him, and chucked him out.''

"So he hates women, is that it?''

"Haw! Well, he don't hate you, thet's fer sure. Ask him yourself. Here he comes now.''

Morty went back to the coach, leaving Lorene alone. Luke came up, carrying his bedroll.

"You ready to ride?'' he asked.

"I'll go *wherever* you go, Luke,'' she said suggestively, and her voice dripped with promise and desire. He looked at her and tried to fathom the meaning in her sea-green eyes, but there was only a mysterious light and a smile on her lips that made him go weak in the knees—made him blame the weakness on his wound and the loss of blood.

"I'll get my horse,'' he gruffed and stalked away, her smile mocking him every step.

"Squaw, indeed!'' Lorene said under her breath.

Nearly three hours after leaving the stagecoach, and

several miles after passing the carnage at the site of the burned-out eastbound stage, Luke and Lorene approached the way station at Cow Spring, prepared for the worst.

Cow Spring, like many of the other stations along the stage route, had a single tent for the accommodation of the stationmen and where the passengers could eat simple fare out of the glare of the sun. When Luke and Lorene rode up, the tent flap was open, but there was no sign of life.

"You'd better wait here while I ride in and see if anyone's about," he told her.

"Are you trying to spare my sensibilities?" she asked, her copper hair brilliant in the sun, somehow giving her a cool look despite the late-morning heat.

"The Apaches might have been here, too," he said, his eyes scanning the surrounding plain.

"After what we have seen today, there isn't much that could shock me, Mr. Faraday. I'll ride over there with you."

"Suit yourself," he said curtly. They had not lingered long at the burned-out stage, but he had observed her closely while he was checking the markings on the arrows. She had looked at the dead people and had not cringed. Yet the stench was enough to make his own stomach turn over. Lorene had sat on her horse until he was finished, her face shaded by a wide-brimmed hat Morty had given her when they left the stage at Cookes Pass.

The markings on the arrows had told Luke much about the Apaches. He found where they had waited, flanking the trail and catching the stage as it pulled up a grade. Ten braves, no more, and they had headed northwest— in a hurry, as if they had a prearranged destination. While the bodies had been mutilated, they had not been robbed. The braves were traveling light, and they weren't carrying loot back to a camp. Pistols were missing, and a broken rifle had been exchanged for a better one carried on the stage. The rifle left behind was decorated with a feather and with brass tacks hammered into the stock. The stock had been repaired with leather soaked and then drawn tight by the drying effects of the sun.

Luke rode up to the way-station tent and dismounted.

As he stepped into the tent, Lorene swung to the ground and wrapped her reins around the hitch rail.

There was no one inside the tent, no blood, no signs of a struggle. But the corral was empty, and Luke found spilled flour and salt that told him someone had taken provisions and left in a hurry.

Lorene looked at him sharply as he came out of the tent, but he ignored her, making a wide circle of the area and squatting on his haunches at one place. She came up to him as he traced a print in the soft dirt.

"What happened here?" she asked him.

"Something scared off the stationmen. Apaches. The stationmen waited until they left and then took some flour and salt, maybe some fatback. This is a moccasin track. Over there, a dozen unshod ponies stood awhile. These are a couple of days old—a day old, maybe. Wind would have taken them away except for that hump in the land along here."

"You know all that from the tracks." It was a flat statement. She accepted it.

"I guess at a lot, too," he said, standing up.

His face darkened, and his pale eyes smoked. She saw the look and wondered. Luke took off his hat and scratched his head. He walked around, looking at the ground, saying nothing. He scanned the empty plain and the ridges as if silently asking the earth itself to answer the question in his mind.

Finally, he returned to the tent. Lorene followed inside and poked around the grub box, examining the iron stove. A kangaroo rat startled her as it ran from behind a can of lard.

"Look," he said, "the Apaches have already been here. They likely won't be back. We've got a hard ride to Apache Pass, and the horses are tuckered. Might be best to rest here awhile and have a bite to eat."

"Your leg is hurting you, isn't it?"

"Some."

"But there's something else bothering you besides that."

"Bodine didn't come by here."

"No?"

"Either he saw Apaches this way or he's pushing on. I missed the place where he left the trail. I got careless."

"Maybe he's behind us and hasn't gotten this far."

"No. He's got that gal and he'll likely take her to Fort Yuma to get her father to let Chet Morgan out of prison."

"He must have been the one who took Chastity's letters and her photograph."

"Can you manage grub? Something light. If we hit the road soon, we can reach one or two stations before dark."

"I can manage." Lorene laughed as a thought crossed her mind. "If Anne Jenkins, that busybody, could see us now, she'd really be upset. She made some remarks to me before we rode off together. She thinks I'm a rather loose woman to go off with you like this."

"It might give people something to talk about."

"You don't mind?"

"People have to talk about something. A reputation isn't much—just gloss. Nobody knows what's inside a person."

"No," she said, looking at him sharply, "one never knows what a person is really like. Even when a man says he's married and really isn't, he's probably got his reasons for telling a fib."

"I'll tend to the horses," Luke said gruffly, hurrying from the tent. "No sense in keeping them under saddle."

Lorene's soft laughter followed him out of the tent into the late-morning glare.

Two miles after hurrying past the burned-out stage from Yuma, Morty Tubbs felt one of the coach's front wheels giving way—the wheel that had given them trouble all the way from El Paso. The wobble shook the coach, shivering his seat. The coach lurched, and he heard a spoke snap.

"Whoa!" he yelled, grabbing for the brake.

The team felt the weight shift and swung to the right. The left front wheel, freed of pressure, slid along the shaft. Morty hauled in hard on the reins, and the horses stopped fighting the bits. The wheel, canted at a thirty-degree angle, took the weight again, and spokes splintered like toothpicks. The coach tilted, and the passengers were thrown against the low side. The wheel broke at the rim, and one side of the coach came down with a sickening crash.

Anne Jenkins screamed. Cornwallis bellowed. Merle Jenkins cursed. "Damned driver up there!"

Stuart Gorman slammed into Morty, nearly knocking him from his perch. Morty hung on for a minute, then slid off the seat like butter across a hot skillet. He hit the ground with a thud, tumbled off-balance, and sprawled in the dirt.

Stuart, bracing himself on his seat, looked down at him.

"I—I'm sorry, Morty," he said.

"Ain't no never mind." But when he got up, he was limping. "Twisted my danged ankle is all. Jump down, son, we got us a wheelwright's job to get to."

Gingerly, Gorman climbed down as the passengers spilled out of the teetering coach.

"Now what?" asked Jenkins.

"Well, look at the danged wheel, mister," said Tubbs, annoyed. "You folks might jes' as well stretch your legs. Young Gorman and I'll tend to the wheel."

"You will never fix that wheel," observed Cornwallis. He straightened his rumpled clothing, pulled his whiskey flask from his coat pocket, and took a swig. "Not unless you carry carpenter's tools."

"I do and I can, but we ain't gonna fix that'n. Stuart, you reckon you can hike back to that burned-out stage and wrestle a wheel loose?"

"If you tell me what to do," Gorman said, beaming. He was glad to be of use after knocking Morty from the seat.

"I'll get the tools and come with you. Mebbe my

ankle ain't so bad." Morty walked around, testing it; it wasn't so bad. When they had quickly passed the east-bound stage and gone on, Morty had noticed the wheels were intact—at least two of them. It would not be pleasant work and the other wheel wouldn't be a perfect fit, but it would take him two days to rebuild the wheel that was broken. He had the tools to repair it, but it would mean using a lot of wires and splints, with no guarantee they'd get very far. "You folks make yourselves comfortable and take some lunch. It's almost noon, and it'll be a long time past when we reach the next station. Stu and I've got a heap of work to do."

"Well, I never . . ." scowled Anne. "If this isn't outrageous!"

Morty ignored her as he dug tools out of the boot. Gorman, eager to help, grabbed them as fast as Morty found them, until his hands were filled with hammer, maul, pliers, rope, and wedge.

"See if the lieutenant's all right," Morty told Jenkins. "He'll bake inside that coach. See if you can find him some shade. This part of the day's hotter'n the hinges of hell."

Jenkins glowered at Morty, but a look from Cornwallis made him hold his tongue.

Stack groaned from inside the coach, and Anne went to see what she could do. Meanwhile, Morty and Stuart evened up their load and started hiking back to the other stage.

Cornwallis watched them go, then pulled Jenkins aside. "I want to talk to you, Merle. Get that horse soldier settled and meet me out of earshot."

"You could help, too, Hiram."

Cornwallis glared at Jenkins, drew himself up in a pose of self-importance, and walked away from the coach.

Stack was wedged in on the low side of the compart-ment. Merle and Anne helped him out of the coach and brought him around to the other side where there was a patch of shade. Anne gave him water and put a pillow under his head. He thanked her and closed his eyes.

"Stay with him," Merle said. "Cornwallis wants to talk."

Anne's look warned him that he might have said too much in front of the trooper.

"Well, I don't give a damn anymore. Hiram's getting under my skin. That drunk act, his damned suspicions. I told you he was going to be trouble."

"Merle, we need him, for a while."

He left her and walked over to where Cornwallis stood in the shade of some boulders beside the road.

"What is it, Hiram?" Jenkins wiped sweat from his forehead, dabbed at his chin.

"That stage from Yuma. Quite disconcerting. Those men, the women. Most gruesome sight I've ever seen. I surmise that this was the work of your friend, Mangas Sangrías.

"Dammit, Hiram, he's not my friend. I made a deal with him—traded those rifles to get him on our side. You know all that."

"But you said nothing about a stage itself being attacked. What if that red-skinned scoundrel decides to do the same to the one we're riding?"

Cornwallis was perspiring profusely. His eyes were dulled from the heat and worry. Jenkins enjoyed seeing the congressman do a little sweating. The man was desperate, and it was beginning to show. While he was still a member of Congress, he was a valuable ally—but there was no trusting the man. He went the way the wind blew, and that was that.

"Mangas will be well paid for his work. We have to prove that Butterfield can't handle this line. I think we're doing that. Mangas was supposed to run off all the stationmen and hit the eastbound stage. Bodine, too, is playing right into our hands. Taking that girl won't set well with the postmaster general or the Eastern interests."

"But you never told me what kind of fiend this Mangas is. Putting rifles in the hands of such a wild savage is like putting a fox in the hen house, Merle. And you still haven't answered my question. What's to prevent this Apache from shooting us all dead? After all, he doesn't like us, and he's extremely dangerous.''

"More rifles, Hiram. I promised him more rifles and ammunition at the end of the run to Fort Yuma. If he kills us now, he won't get them.''

"Where will those rifles come from?''

"San Francisco. I realize they're not as good as those Spencer repeaters you delivered, but he'll be satisfied. I don't expect Mangas to live much longer, anyway. The army will track him down soon enough.''

Suddenly the congressman's features hardened into stone. "I'm going to have to get rid of young Gorman.''

"How? When?''

"When the time is right. And I'll want that packet Miss Martin stuck in her saddlebag when she rode off with that Faraday fellow. Those papers must never reach San Francisco. I need time if I'm to be of help to you.''

"Well, maybe something can be worked out.''

Their conversation was interrupted by Anne Jenkins, who was waving at them from the coach.

"Something's up,'' said Jenkins. "Just don't do anything rash, Hiram. Let me decide how to get those papers and take care of Gorman.''

"Just don't wait too long, Merle. My nerves can't stand much more of this!''

Anne waved more furiously now and pointed off into the distance. And then Cornwallis and Jenkins saw what she was indicating. It was a lone rider, approaching slowly out of the north.

Morty finished stacking the last flat rock under the hulk of the stage from Yuma. Another lay ready.

"You'll have to get your back under there and lift, son. Think you're up to it?''

"Yes, sir.''

For the last half hour the two had sweated, gathering rocks to hold the stage up off the ground so they could remove the wheel. The last rock would be placed on top of the stack once Stuart got the stage lifted. They had no lever pole, and the stage didn't have a jack.

Stuart crawled under the coach and braced his back against the leaf springs. Morty picked up the rock, holding it ready.

"Don't move the stage sideways if you can help it, son. When I give you the sign, put the strain on your legs and push up with your back. Ready?"

"Anytime."

Morty nodded, and Stuart strained. The coach moved slightly. Stuart grunted and pushed harder. Quickly, Morty shoved the rock under the axle.

"Now let 'er down gentle."

The rocks quivered, but held. Stuart scrambled from under the coach.

"Good strong lad. Now fetch me them tools and we'll take that wheel."

The stench of death was overpowering, but Morty worked fast. He removed the wheel after bending down the cotter pin and hammering it free. Just as he wrenched the wheel off the axle, the stack of rocks gave way.

"Look out!" shouted Gorman.

Morty fell away with the wheel as the coach came down hard on axle and springs. The coach tipped, hurling the dead driver from the seat. Something fell from the man's coat. Stuart instinctively reached for it and picked it up.

Morty untangled himself from the wagon wheel and dusted himself off. "What ya got there, son?"

Gorman turned the leather packet over in his hands. "I don't know. It fell out of that man's pocket."

"Lemme see." Morty hobbled over and took the leather pouch from Gorman. "It's a special dispatch pouch. That's Harvey Nickles, the driver. Must've been mighty important." Morty opened the pouch and withdrew the papers.

"Warrants," said Gorman, recognizing the official headings.

"And copies of a wanted poster. Picture on it, too. For delivery to any U.S. marshal."

"The name," said Stuart. "Look at it. Merle Jeffries. And that's a picture of . . ."

He didn't have to finish the words. They both could plainly see the posters bore an exact likeness of Merle Jenkins. And he was wanted for bribery and conspiracy.

"Son, you didn't see anything. Don't say a word about this till we reach Yuma. It's a long trail 'twixt here and there, and it'll go smoother if he don't know we've seen this. We'll let the army handle it at the fort."

Stuart whistled as Morty stuffed the pouch inside his shirt. "Morty, Congressman Cornwallis is in with him. I know it."

"Son, you got to make a choice, and it ain't gonna be easy. I been watching you. You've got some stuff in you, some backbone. I can't help you make up your mind, but one of these days you're either gonna have to cross the river or stay on that politician's payroll."

Stuart stood up straight, looking Morty square in the eye. "I've already made up my mind, Mr. Tubbs. I've seen two kinds of men—those in Washington and those out here. There's a lot of difference. And I guess I'm learning a lot about honesty and character and breeding."

"By cracky, Stuart, you talk like a feller I knowed a long time ago when he come out west, tryin' to make up his own mind."

"Who's that?"

"Luke Faraday. Now let's get on back."

The lone horseman pulled up in front of Cornwallis and the Jenkins couple at the stage. He was in bad shape—thirsty, frightened, almost raving. Merle helped him from his horse to a place beside Lieutenant Stack. His name was Pat Foster, and he said he was the stationmaster at Cow Spring.

"Mangas come by, run off all the horses but one, this 'un."

Foster lay panting in the shade. Stack sat up, listening to his story. The others hovered against the coach, watching the man gulp water and talk between swallows.

"Injuns pulled back, but they was watching the road east and west. Only way out was to the north or south. I cut north, then east and south back to the stage road."

"Did you see any other riders?" Stack asked. "Four men and a woman? Or a man and a woman trailing them?"

"Nobody. I jes' rode like hell north, till I figgered it was safe to cut back. And it was mighty strange."

"Strange? What was?" Stack asked.

"The horse. Mangas coulda took them all. But he left this one, like he wanted me to get away. He's crazy, all right. Raising smoke all along the stage route. I jes' hope that eastbound got through. The driver, Harvey Nickles, was carryin' special papers. Warrants for the arrest of an easterner name of Jeffries."

"Well, he didn't make it," said Stack. "The Apaches hit the stage just east of here."

Merle Jenkins had frozen at the mention of his real name. He exchanged looks with Cornwallis and Anne.

Tubbs and Gorman were at the burned-out stage. If they found those papers, he'd have to kill them both. He drew a breath.

Cornwallis nodded and drew a finger across his throat. The two men understood each other perfectly now.

Pat Foster scrambled to his feet. "I'll be off now. And if I was you, I'd do the same. Turn back east. To the west there's nothing but Apaches . . . and death."

"But . . ." And before Stack could finish his thought, the phantom rider was atop his horse and gone, driven by the same demons that were haunting every mile of this stagecoach journey to Fort Yuma.

Chapter 8

The sky was a scrawl of color, daubs of gray, a swirl of gold where the sun had gone down. Shadows streaked the rosy land, deepened in the arroyos, blackened the massive east faces of the red buttes.

Bodine and his men were far from the road, riding through the rocks and seeking shelter. It had been a long, slow day of riding, made the more intolerable by the oppressive heat and the need to take turns riding double with Chastity Blaine. Now, after skirting the Cow Spring way station and charting a more direct route to Apache Pass along a line south of the stage road, the ragged group had at last reached this area of scrubby rock hills somewhere south of Stein's Peak—less than a day's ride from Apache Pass.

"There's a cave up there," Dan Rawlings said as he pointed to the rocks above them. "Might be water in the crannies."

"We'll hole up then," said Bodine, "and ride for Apache Pass in the morning."

No one said anything. Peeker's eyes were slitted, his cheekbones raw from sunburn. Rawlings led them through the rocks on a narrow game trail. Chastity rocked in the saddle behind Rafe Adams, her body aching in every joint, her flesh burning from the heat of the sun. Her legs were chafed where her dress had rubbed, and her hair was heavy with sand and grit.

Erosion from wind and rain had hollowed out a large natural shelter in the rock. As they approached the cave, Chastity felt a sudden tremor of fear. The realization struck her that she would spend the night alone with four men, rough men who cared little for her comfort or feelings. The man they called Peeker had been ogling her all day, and once when he had ridden close, his hand had reached out and touched her leg. She remembered this with a shudder as the sunset sky continued to darken and shadows deepened inside the cave.

Rafe and Bodine dismounted and began to unsaddle. Peeker rode up to Rawlings, and the two men slid from their saddles. Rawlings put his hands around Chastity's waist and lifted her to the ground.

"You behave, miss," he said. "Ain't none of us would think twice about shootin' you if you try to run away."

"Where would I run?" she asked defiantly.

Peeker guffawed. Rawlings looked out over the vast plain and began to laugh, too. "That's right," he said. "Where would you run? There's nothin' but rattlesnakes and Injuns out there."

"I might be safer with them at that," she retorted.

Peeker's eyes slitted again. "Don't you get too smart," he said to her. "I don't like smart-aleck gals."

The men lugged saddles, blankets, and bedrolls into the cave. Rawlings forced Chastity to sit inside, where he could keep an eye on her.

Chastity watched the men as they stowed their gear and checked their weapons. The light hung on the high ground and the peaks of hills. She saw their weariness begin to match her own as they grumbled and moved about with shuffling steps and sagging shoulders. Peeker's slit-eyes raked her every time he passed, until she felt as if mites were crawling all over her flesh—as if her clothes were being slowly peeled from her body, exposing her to his merciless gaze.

After Peeker finished stacking his gear, he sauntered to where Chastity sat and plunked himself down beside her. She cringed and tried to inch away. The outlaw shot a hand out, clawed her arm, and pulled her toward him.

"You ain't goin' nowheres, missy."

"Leave me alone!"

His fingers dug into the fleshy muscle below her shoulder. He tugged her closer, leaning over so that his face was but a few inches from hers. His breath was hot against her cheek. She winced, and his fingers tightened again.

"You—you're hurting me," she gasped.

"Jest give a man a little kiss, huh?"

She twisted her head as he shoved his face forward. His other hand lashed out like a whip, grabbing her other shoulder. He jerked her torso toward him and forced his lips onto hers. She tasted the stale heat from his mouth. She heard his hard breathing and felt the smothering heat of his embrace. The thought of what her teacher back east had said to her flashed across her mind: *It is not proper for a young lady to travel out west alone, despite what your father says. You must have a chaperone, and the school will provide one for the appropriate fee.*

Yet her father had insisted that she would be perfectly safe on the stage line, since the army was always close at hand. The bitter irony of her father's stinginess impressed itself upon her once again—as Peeker's mouth crushed against hers, as his weight bore her down onto the floor of the cave.

"Hey, Peeker," said Rawlings, coming over to them. "You jumped the gun a mite, didn't you?"

"Keep outa my corral," growled Peeker, breaking his kiss. He ripped at the bodice of Chastity's dress, trying to bare her breasts. His eyes filled with light and wetness, his nostrils flared with desire.

"Stop it!" a voice shouted.

Peeker straddled her and began working at his belt buckle.

"Leave her alone!" Rafe Adams stepped into the cave.

"Hell, we just gonna have her one time apiece," said Rawlings. "Peeker won't be a minute!" And he laughed.

"I said leave her alone. We want her pretty, not all marked up by you two mules."

Peeker twisted to face Adams. "Don't press me, Rafe."

Bodine stepped out of the fading light to stand next to Adams. "*I'll* damn sure press you if you don't get your ass off'n that gal."

For a long moment, no one moved. Chastity held her breath. She could hear Peeker's breathing—low, shallow, staccato.

Then he moved. His weight lifted and she could breathe freely again.

"Hell, Bodine, mebbe you want her first. Go right ahead."

"You heard Rafe. She's merchandise. A trade. Worth money to us. We can't risk messin' the deal with her pa."

"He'll never know," Rawlings countered.

"He might. Hell, she might come apart and turn loco, from the likes of you two climbin' all over her. And that pa of hers is jest the kinda bastard that wouldn't want her back iffen he thought she was soiled goods. So you two jest hold on. After I spring Morgan, you can do what you want with her."

"You mean you ain't gonna give her to Blaine?"

Bodine looked at Chastity and grinned. She felt a chill brush over her flesh as if someone had taken the sharp edge of a knife and held it to her throat.

"I'm gonna kill her pa," Bodine said. "Jest as soon as he turns Morgan over to me."

Fort Yuma was a place nobody wanted to be. The army had abandoned its fort there in 1853. The prison that took its place was a cruel afterthought—something devised by bureaucratic minds who sought to sweep waste under a rug of sand and yucca and make someone pay for the army's foolishness at having built the fort in the first place. Or perhaps they hated mankind so much that they leaped upon the chance to turn an abandoned fort into a prison for men who could not fight back.

What the army had designed as a fortress was now an oven that baked men's souls as it fried their brains. Escape was most often futile because of the prison's location—it was miles from civilization, and men who climbed over the walls often came back voluntarily, their tongues burnt black from thirst, their eyes stark in their sockets, their flesh bitten by thousands of invisible insects and reptiles that slithered in the night across the desolate wasteland.

Originally established as Fort Independence on November 27, 1850, the fort was moved in March of the following year to a low hill on the west bank of the Colorado River, into the old Mission Puerto de la Purísima Concepción. The mission earlier had served as the site of Camp Calhoun, named for former Vice President John C. Calhoun, and had been established on October 2, 1849, to protect a boundary survey party of the Corps of Topographical Engineers.

After moving to the mission, the fort was ordered to be shut down in June 1851 because of the expense and difficulty of keeping it supplied, but it continued to struggle along until December 6, 1851, when the supplies ran out and the soldiers left. Captain Samuel P. Heintzelman, Second U.S. Infantry, reoccupied the fort on February 29, 1852, and christened it Fort Yuma.

Fort Yuma existed to protect the southern emigrant route to California and to act as a buffer against the marauding Yuma Indian bands that periodically swarmed over the region. After the Yuma were driven back and suppressed, the fort served as a supply depot for army posts in Arizona.

When the fort again was abandoned by the army in 1853, one section of the old adobe mission was reinforced, bars were set into the thick walls, an iron gate was installed, and the prison was born. After the Overland Mail Company began regular service on September 16, 1858, the fort and the prison took on new life, with the army again maintaining a presence to protect the stage line. Now, a year later, Vernon Blaine was acting warden. On this Monday evening, Blaine had reason to gloat: A rider from El Paso had ridden in that afternoon with the news of Ernie Bodine's capture in El Paso.

Chet Morgan stood before Blaine's desk, his feet shackled, his wrists in irons. The coarse linen clothes hung on his frame like patched-together shrouds. His face bristled with beard, and his tobacco-stained teeth showed behind curled-back lips. His dark eyes glistened under overhanging brows. He was lean and deceptively strong from constant exercise, and his short-cropped black hair scarcely concealed the scars from beatings administered by guards and prisoners alike. Morgan was hated because he knew where the army payroll was hidden and would not tell.

Blaine hated him merely because he was a prisoner, a man without defenses and without friends. Godless.

"Bodine didn't last long, did he, Morgan?"

"He ain't here yet."

"He's coming, though. Sure as sin, he's coming on the next Overland."

Vernon Blaine was short, small boned, fair haired, and blue eyed—like his daughter, Chastity. His eyes, however, were pins stuck into a bony skeletal face, set too close together under a wide, glistening forehead. His lips were thin wet strips pasted on a chalky face. He was aware of his short stature: his desk was mounted on a wooden platform, and his chair was oversized. He looked down at Morgan with contempt, deftly manipulating a gleaming letter opener to catch the morning sun and reflect it, every so often, into Morgan's eyes. Now, flashing the light at Morgan's face, Blaine was angry because the prisoner didn't flinch or try to shade his eyes. Instead, Morgan looked up with those bared-back lips at the skull head of the warden, as if ready to pounce. Two guards stood close at hand, bored with the ritual they had seen performed so many times since Blaine had taken over the prison.

Morgan seethed but said nothing.

"You listening, Morgan? Bodine's going to hang

with you, just like the judge said. He's coming in on the stage at three in the morning Friday. By noon, you'll both be swinging.''

"Blaine, you got the heart of a pig!"

The acting warden stiffened, his eyes seeming to draw back in their sockets until they were as hard as nail heads. Then, he leaned forward, confidentially.

"Morgan, you still got a chance to escape the hangman's noose. You tell me where you buried that payroll, and I'll put in a good word for you with the judge. We can get your sentence commuted. Hell, you don't owe Bodine nothing. Why swing on his account? Why, I could even make you a trusty—help you get a parole in a couple years.''

Morgan pretended to consider Blaine's offer. He looked down at his wrist shackles, then up at the warden.

"You want me to tell you where we hid the money?"

"That's right, Morgan.'' Blaine's lips slavered as he leaned forward over his desk. "Just tell me where it's buried. I'll take care of the rest.''

Morgan's lips curled back even farther. "Why don't you kiss my ass, Blaine,'' he said quietly.

Blaine rose from his chair, his eyes boiling with fury, pushing from their sockets as if about to explode from his skull. "Quinlan!'' he barked.

One of the guards came forward, pulling a small wooden truncheon from his waistband. Quinlan's arm lifted. Morgan didn't flinch as the truncheon came down on his shoulder. He sagged, but remained on his feet.

Blaine came around from the desk, slobber on his lips. "Hit him in the head!'' he shrieked.

Morgan ducked the second blow and rushed the warden. He lashed out with manacled hands, fingers straining to find the man's windpipe and crush it. The second guard dashed forward as Blaine struck out with the letter opener, stabbing at Morgan's grasping hands. Quinlan waded in, swinging his truncheon. Just as Morgan's fingers grasped Blaine's coat collar, the guard jabbed his stick into Morgan's back, striking the right kidney with a vicious blow. Morgan went down.

"Kill him! Kill him!" screamed Blaine.

The guards beat Morgan down, bloodying his head, bruising ribs and arms.

Blaine's fingers were white on the letter opener, drained from squeezing the object in his fury. "Wait," Blaine said, recovering his composure. "Enough! Throw him back in his cell. He'll hang. Oh, he'll hang like a butchered hog!"

The guards lifted the unconscious Morgan by his arms and dragged him from the office.

Blaine wiped the slobber from his mouth and stood there for a long time, trembling with hatred and impotence.

Chet Morgan woke to an insistent tapping. His head throbbed, and his shoulder felt as if it had been bent, if not broken. His ribs churned with pain every time he took a breath. Dizzy, groggy from the beating, he took in his surroundings. It was night, but the cell still smoked with the pent-up heat of the day. The thick walls were scummed with spittle, mashed roaches and flies, and lizard slime. A scorpion scuttled across the far end, its tail arched as if asking a question.

The tapping had a pattern to it.

"Morgan?" The voice came from the next cell— throaty, a whispered shout.

"Yeah?"

"You been out for over an hour."

"Yeah. Safe to talk? I got news." Morgan staggered to his feet, sending the scorpion burrowing under the wall as he lurched to the iron door. There he could speak through a crack to the man in the neighboring cell. Leaning close to the crack, they could see each other's faces and lips, a sliver of skin.

"Listen, Arnie," said Morgan. "Blaine said they caught Bodine."

"I know," said Arneson, a civilian convicted of murdering his partner in a dispute over a woman. "Word's out there'll be a double hanging on Friday."

"Bodine's coming in on the stage. We got to meet it."

"We're all set."

"You take care of the guard?"

"He's paid off—the pistols are smuggled in. We're just waiting for the word."

Morgan wiped the sweat out of his eyes—it stung, and he could not see for a moment. The moonlight filtered through a small high window, giving the cell a ghostly cast.

"Tomorrow night," husked Morgan. "It has to be Tuesday. Pass the word. We go when they bring the chow around."

"Where we going, Chet?"

"First we head off that stage and get Bodine loose. That'll mean more money for all of us."

"Then what?"

"Then we ride for that payroll I got buried. But we got to beat that stage, savvy?"

"I savvy," said Arneson.

"Pass the word. Tomorrow night. Chowtime."

A gate clanged, keys jangled. Morgan slid to the floor, exhausted. The guard's steps sounded muted through the iron door—strangely disembodied. They stopped, then continued on.

Morgan grinned, his lips curling back like a smiling wolf's. He moved his hand, cupping it around an imaginary pistol. He hammered it back, raised it, sighted down the invisible barrel. In front of him danced the face of Vernon Blaine. Chuckling to himself, Morgan squeezed the trigger. His mouth made a sound like an explosion—a sound he hadn't uttered since he was a kid, playing with a wooden toy pistol back in Kentucky. His laughter filled the cell.

"Shut up!" yelled the guard.

And Morgan lifted the phantom gun and shot him, too, just for good measure.

*   *   *

As the moon rose higher above the stage road just
east of Cookes Pass, Mangas Sangrías kneed his pinto past
the arrow of rocks to the mound of earth beyond. His face
was a burnished sheet of copper, hammered into a mask.
Streaks of vermilion, ocher, and chalk broke up the bronze
mask, giving his eyes a fierce look, his mouth a cruel
shape.

"Solamente dos cajas," he muttered in Spanish.

"Ho," said Corto, one of the men scooping away the
sand. "Only two boxes."

Two men dug where Jenkins and Cornwallis had
cached the rifles, while half a dozen Apaches looked on
with solemn eyes.

"These are the rifles that shoot many times," said
Corto. "We do not need so many."

"We will see," said Mangas.

When the boxes were removed, the chief ordered them
opened. He sat his pony very still, his headband a crimson
bandanna, his moccasins dangling under his pony's belly.
He wore a breechcloth, with no shirt. His arms were
banded with colors. The wizened scowl on his face seemed
permanently etched into his flesh.

The two braves forced the boxes open, splintering
wood with their heavy knives. One of them pried a rifle
loose and held it up. He took it to Mangas. When the rifle
was placed in Mangas's hand, his arm went down under
the weight.

"Cabrón," he cursed.

The other braves swarmed over the boxes, jerking
rifles into their hands. Some hefted tins of black powder
and ball. There were two brass molds. They bitterly exclaimed in both Apache and Spanish about the large caliber of the bullets and bores of the rifles.

"Cagada!" said Corto. "No good!"

The rifles were Enfield muzzle-loaders, made in
England. Each was a hefty eight and a half pounds, forty-
eight inches long, and .58 caliber. Mangas tried to swing
his rifle back and forth, up and down. He galloped his

pony in a circle, guiding him with his knees, as he brought the rifle up to his shoulder and tried to aim. The rifle was extremely unwieldy and almost impossible to use on horseback.

"He lied, this white man Jenkins," observed Corto. "These are not rifles that shoot many times."

Mangas drew his horse up short and threw the rifle down. It struck stone, clattering as it slid off into the sand beside the road. The other braves froze like statues.

Mangas looked over their heads, down the trail, toward the far passes that he could not see. Some time ago a man had come to him, one of those who spoke the tongues. He was a small man, more white than Apache, but he had a blood mother and so he was listened to—even though there were those who did not like such *mezclas*, such mixings. This man spoke of rifles that could shoot many times without putting powder down the barrel after every shot. He spoke of a white man who could give them such rifles. All that white man wanted was for the Apaches to drive off the white eyes who had the stage stations. This was good talk, and Mangas was glad to have such an ally among white men.

The days of the Apache were numbered now that so many soldiers had come into the land and set up forts to guard and protect the settlers. But the Apache lands were still there, away from these trails and towns, if only the soldiers would leave them alone to hunt and roam. The Mexicans were no longer a problem, nor a challenge.

But this man, Jenkins, wanted the white eyes driven away for a time, and he promised magic rifles. Rifles that would shoot many times. Rifles that would defeat the bluecoats, who had no such weapons. Now, Mangas knew, neither did Jenkins. It was all a lie. Another white man's lie.

Mangas looked at the rifle lying in the dust. It was a new rifle, unfired. Better than any they had. But it was like shooting with a tree trunk. It was no good for them. Their ponies were fast, and his people could ride well, but with these rifles they would die in their saddles.

"These guns are no good," he announced.

"They are big killing guns," said Brown Root, a young man of twenty summers.

"They are like spears for buffalo," said Corto. "You cannot kill rabbits with them."

"A charging rat would eat you up before you could reach the end of such a stick to load it," said another, going along with the feeling.

"The rifles are heavy."

"It takes much metal to cast a bullet," said another.

Mangas listened to them, and he heard his own thoughts echoed.

The Apaches spoke their minds until they heard one of their scouts riding hard to them with a report. Mangas saw the man coming and held up his hand for silence. It had been agreed that the rifles would be kept, because they were weapons, but none of the braves wanted to be the first to load and fire one of the big guns.

Mano Mojada—Wet Hand—reined up, jerking hard on the horsehair bridle. His pony skidded to a stop in front of Mangas. "Four white men, one woman stolen from the big carry-wagon, ride for Apache Pass. One white man and a white woman follow."

"The carry-wagon?"

"It follows, too."

"So the man Bodine has captured a prisoner."

"*Una rubia*, very fair young girl."

"They will not make the pass tonight," said Mangas.

"No. They made camp. They reach the pass before the sun sleeps tomorrow."

Mangas looked at the men around him. "I do not trust this Jenkins. He has given us bad rifles. His tongue is black with lies. His heart is bad. We should kill this man and the others. If we do this, there will be no more carry-wagons on this road. The soldiers will go away. I believe this."

A chorus of assenting grunts testified to the willingness of the Apache braves to go along with their leader.

"Soldiers are east where the sun rises. We have

driven off the white men in the carry-wagon camps. If we ride fast we can wait for all the white eyes in Apache Pass. Mano, you will bring all the other bands of warriors there. Change your horse with Corto. His is fresh and will carry you fast.''

''Hunnh!''

There was blood in Mangas's eyes as he led his own men toward the pass. Some called it Doubtful Pass. Others called it Apache Pass. It amounted to the same thing: If the Apaches were there, it was doubtful anyone could get through.

And Mangas would be there before the sun set on another day.

Chapter 9

Chastity Blaine awoke with a start. The cave was gray with light. A large shape loomed above her. Again she felt the toe of a boot prod her in the side. She shivered in the morning cold, sat up, and looked around for the men. Only Ernie Bodine was there.

"Get up," he said. "You ride with me."

"I'm hungry," she said defiantly.

He reached down, grabbed her hair, and pulled her to her feet.

"Get outside," he said curtly.

Chastity stumbled, half asleep, to the cave entrance. The horses were saddled. A cigarette glowed in the hands of Will Peeker. In the east, a pale cream light glowed in the sky. Bodine left her and walked over to Rafe Adams.

"The gal will ride with me," he said. "I want you to ride ahead."

Adams squinted, sniffing the air. "Injuns been ridin' all night," he said. "Still dust hangin' in the air."

"I know. Reckon where they be headed?" asked Bodine.

"Apache Pass?"

"Maybe. How many you figger?"

Adams swung around, scanning the land below. He had heard the hoofbeats of unshod horses after midnight, and every so often after that—small bunches, coming from different directions. Once he had thought he'd seen campfires winking in the dark. And he had seen a glow in the sky beyond Stein's Peak just before dawn. Shortly after that, a band of Indians had passed close enough for him to smell them. His eyes hurt now from lack of sleep, from peering into the dark and challenging every shadow, every startling sound.

"Small bunches, but all headed the same direction. Thirty—forty, maybe. At least a dozen come from Stein's Peak."

"We got to go through that pass, Rafe."

"We might make it in a run. But it would be suicide to go through there ridin' double."

Chastity caught Rafe's look and bit her lip. She knew what they were thinking: She was expendable. She could almost smell their fear. Her own fear was fuming inside her, strangling her, yet she refused to let it erupt. The men had grumbled about her last night, but they had left her alone because Bodine had slept near her. Yet that same fear was now transformed as she realized that she had far worse things to be afraid of than mistreatment at the hands of these outlaws. Bodine was sobered by Rafe's report, and Rafe himself was worried more than he cared to show. His words seemed to catch in his throat, and his hand was never very far away from his holstered pistol.

"We got to take her, Rafe." Bodine's look went to Peeker, who was nervously puffing on his cigarette, which was flattened and damp with his saliva, so that he had to draw hard to bring smoke into his lungs.

"Well, Ernie, you might have to make a choice somewheres down the line," Rafe continued. "I sure as hell don't know what so many Apaches are doin', makin' smoke talk and ridin' like that in the night, but whatever it is, it ain't no good for nobody."

"Could be the army's chasin' 'em," volunteered Peeker.

"You think that?" asked Rafe. "Then you don't

know Injuns. Them Apaches are plumb primed for trouble. They're riding *to* something, not *from* something.''

Rawlings put a hand on Peeker's shoulder, as if to keep him from saying any more. Peeker whirled on him, flicking the butt of his cigarette toward the cave.

"He's right, Will," said Rawlings. "I seen war parties gettin' together a time or two. Like birds gatherin' afore a storm. Same spooky feelin'.''

"Hell, the Apaches won't make war! Army's got Apache scouts now and kin track 'em down.''

Bodine flattened a place in the dirt with the sole of his boot. He made a line across it. "Mangas is stirred up about somethin'," he said. "Maybe about the stage line, maybe over a damned bean patch. Whatever, we got to get through that pass. Now it would be pure fool suicide to ride through there in daylight, so my idea is to snug up to the pass and wait for dark.''

"That pass is plumb hell in the daytime," said Peeker, "and I sure don't aim to go through it blind at night.''

"Rawlings?" asked Bodine. "What about you?"

"Might work. Apaches don't hanker much to fight at night.''

"But they do," said Peeker sullenly.

"Rafe?" Bodine fixed him with a look as if he had the deciding vote.

"If we go through there when the sun's up," he said, "we got thirty or forty Apaches just pickin' us off from both sides. Might be a chance t'sneak through after dark.''

Bodine cracked a wry grin as he looked at Peeker. "We go through real quiet-like, afoot," he said. "Any that don't like it can go through alone in the mornin'.''

Peeker looked at Rafe, then at Rawlings. Neither man made a move. Finally, he looked at Bodine. "They'll hear us sure," he said. "If we're afoot, they'll sneak up on us with knives, 'stead of rifles.''

"It's the only way, Peeker," challenged Bodine. "Make your choice.''

Peeker considered it from all angles. The plan might

work. On foot, they'd be hard targets, and the horses would give them some protection. They might even fool the Apaches. But if Mangas was up there, he'd have some surprises of his own for them. He was smart—and a good fighter. But Indians didn't like waiting all that much. If they went through after dark, their chances would be greater.

"We'll play it your way, Bodine. If they hit us, it's ever' man for hisself anyways."

"Get mounted," said Bodine. "Rafe, you ride ahead. No hurry now. Just get us in sight of that pass, and we'll bed down there until night."

Leather creaked as men climbed into saddles. Bodine reached an arm down for Chastity. She put her foot in the stirrup and felt herself being pulled up. She felt the strength in Bodine's arm, the power in his fingers. She sat behind the cantle, her dress bunched up for protection.

"Stage and posse both might catch up to us." Rawlings said quietly as he rode up beside Bodine. "I'll take the rear on this one."

"Good. And I'll send Peeker back to spell you after a while."

Rawlings nodded and swung his horse around to take up the rear. Rafe rode out ahead. Peeker fell next in line.

"Bodine," Chastity said, her voice scratchy with fear. "Promise me something."

"Yeah?"

"If the Apaches get us, will you shoot me? I—I don't want to be captured by them."

"Gal, if the Apaches get us, I'll shoot us both!"

Just northeast of the cave where Bodine had made camp, Luke Faraday was shaking out his poncho and rolling up his blankets. After leaving Cow Spring at noon, he and Lorene had spent a long day following the stage road west toward Apache Pass, where Luke was certain Bodine was headed.

They had passed by the way station at Soldier's Farewell in the afternoon and had found it abandoned like Cow

Spring. Just before dark, they had reached Stein's Peak Station and had been relieved to find it manned and as yet unbothered by Mangas. There they had stocked up on supplies, exchanged mounts, and then continued on, making camp on the western shoulder of the peak. Now, as the sun rose Tuesday morning, Luke took a few careful steps, testing his leg. The wound had set up some more, and he felt less stiff.

Lorene Martin lifted her head and opened one eye. Her hair was tousled, but she was still beautiful, even by morning light.

"Dawn already?"

"Some past," he replied.

"Why couldn't we have stayed at Stein's Peak last night? In a bed?" She crawled from the blankets, and he thought it had been a shame for her to sleep on hard ground all alone.

"Man lives on hunches out here sometimes. I wondered why nobody was at Soldier's Farewell, yet men were still at the peak. Come here, I'll show you something."

Puzzled, Lorene stood up, placed a hand on her hip, and stretched backward, then to each side. She yawned and ran delicate fingers through her hair. The sun slid over the eastern horizon, and copper light shimmered in her hair. Luke climbed up on a large, flat-topped rock and waited for her. She scrambled up, looking in the direction he pointed—to the east.

"Stein's Peak?"

A pall of smoke hung in the air over the station. A single plume to one side rose straight up.

"Apaches hit it early this morning. And look yonder."

His arm swung around. Far in the distance, she saw strands of dust still hanging in the air—to the north and in the west. Nearer, to the southwest, she saw more dust, and dark specks getting smaller.

"I—I don't understand."

"Apaches, small bunches of them, have been moving west all night long. They hit Stein's Peak and set it afire.

Those other little specks to the southwest will be Bodine and his bunch.''

Lorene strained to see. ''Is—is Chastity with them?''

''Too far to see. But we've got a chance to catch up today. Likely Bodine knows about the Apaches, too. But the only route to Yuma is by way of Apache Pass. He might not make it in daylight.''

''What will we do?''

''I never expected to catch up with him much before the pass. We'll let Bodine have his lead, but keep close. It'll take us all day to catch him as it is. Might be we'll have to ride through the pass after dark.''

Luke helped Lorene climb down from the rock. She felt comfortable with him. Last night she had wanted to talk, and he had listened to her. She was homesick, and seeing those men at Stein's Peak—men who were probably dead now—had made her miss her father, San Francisco, the lush Valley of the Moon, the ranch. Luke had listened, and she had felt his strength, his patience. She had been tempted to touch him, to snuggle up to him, to let him rock her to sleep in his strong arms. But when she finally summoned up the courage to reach out to him, he already had fallen asleep. She could laugh at it now—laugh at how close she had come to surrendering herself to a man she hardly knew.

''Luke, thank you for listening to me last night. You must have thought me a foolish woman.''

''Never. Being alone is not much fun. Too much of it is bad, man or woman.''

''You know, don't you?''

''I can take spells of it.''

''Don't you ever wish for a home of your own? A place where you can go and sit by the fire, take off your boots, and feel safe and loved?''

''I do. But a man gets into habits, and habits are chains—hard to break.''

''Did you ever want to get married?''

He looked at her sharply, but the question was not accusatory. Rather, it was as if she was musing out loud.

"I've thought of it once or twice."

"And?"

Luke laughed. "Heck, I wouldn't know how to ask or who to ask—or how to behave if a lady said yes."

"My guess is you would. If you asked the right lady."

Will Peeker heard a snap, then a sickening crunch. His stomach swirled as the ground fell out from under his horse. He had been half dozing, and now the ground rushed up to meet him. He pitched out of the saddle, trying to brace his fall by throwing up an arm. He kicked free of the stirrups and hit the ground on his left shoulder. His head jarred with pain, and lights danced in front of his eyes.

His horse screamed.

Peeker cursed, rolled over, then sat up. The horse lay thrashing on its side. The others had probably not seen him. He was riding third in line, with Rawlings out front and Bodine and the girl about a quarter mile ahead. Only Rafe was behind. All afternoon he had been riding in their dust, and now this had happened, during a moment of dozing.

Peeker cursed and walked over to the thrashing horse. The animal's eyes were wide, white rimmed, rolling with fear. Stepping around the fallen creature, Peeker saw its left foreleg in the hole. The leg had snapped just above the fetlock. A sliver of bone protruded through the blood-stained hide.

Peeker drew his pistol and cocked it. The explosion shattered the still air. Smoke billowed out from the muzzle of the .44 as the ball sped into the horse's skull. The animal twitched for several moments, its convulsions diminishing to spasms and finally ceasing altogether.

Peeker stripped the animal of its saddle, rifle scabbard, and the pistols hanging from the horn. He kicked the saddle, cursing again.

Bodine and Chastity rode back a few moments later, followed by Rafe Adams. Peeker had already begun to pour powder into the empty cylinder of his revolver. He rammed a ball down, seating it on the powder, and smeared the space over the ball with tallow to prevent chain firing. He set the percussion cap in place and holstered the big Colt.

"Damn fool," said Bodine. "Looks like you done run out of luck, Peeker."

Peeker's face turned chalky with fear and rage. He looked around him at the desolate landscape, the empty sky and the buttes. He looked at Bodine and remembered Bob Johncock. But Bodine made no move for his gun.

"You ain't gonna leave me here, are ya?" he asked.

Bodine laughed mirthlessly.

"Climb up, Peeker," said Rafe, kicking a foot free of a stirrup. "You just might catch yourself one of them Apache ponies."

Peeker gulped and grabbed his rifle and three pistols. He slipped the belts over his shoulders and scrambled up behind Adams.

"Thanks, Rafe. I won't forgit this."

"Git moving," said Bodine. "We're shy two horses, and there's a lot of miles to git."

Peeker didn't look back, but he could feel Bodine's eyes on him, burning into the back of his neck. If there was trouble, he had no doubt Bodine would shoot him without a second thought. Square in the back of the head.

Morty Tubbs saw the smoke long before the stage rumbled up to Stein's Peak Station. The sickly sweet smell of burned human flesh assaulted his nostrils as he set the brake. A glance at the bodies told him all he needed to know. Stuart Gorman, riding shotgun, also saw them, and he leaned over the side of the coach and vomited.

"They didn't bother to scalp 'em," observed Morty. "Just shot 'em and set 'em afire."

Hiram Cornwallis stepped out of the stage, saw Stuart leaning over retching, and climbed back in.

Lieutenant Stack managed to get out the other side.

He was unsteady on his feet, but felt better than he had in two days.

"Well, sir," said Morty, swinging down from his seat, "we can't get fresh horses and we ain't got time for buryin', so I reckon we just rest the horses and go on."

"Apaches?" asked Stack.

"Mimbreños. Mangas's bunch. In a hurry." Morty looked at the tracks, the lieutenant following him as best he could. Moments later, they were joined by Stuart. His face was drained of color, but he showed his gameness by looking at the tracks with Morty and Stack.

"I guess we'd better get out and stretch," said Merle Jenkins.

"The stench is much worse inside," agreed Cornwallis.

"You both are fools," said Anne. "This business has gotten entirely out of hand." She fanned herself with a paper fan brought in anticipation of the heat. Her nostrils flared as her anger rose. She did not have to look out the window. The smell told her what she'd see.

"You're overwrought, my dear," said Merle, trying to mollify her.

"You bet I'm overwrought, Merle! Ever since you botched things with your bid for the mail contract, our life's been in a turmoil. Everyone in New York tried to tell you that the postmaster wanted a southern route, but you wouldn't listen. Butterfield, Bill Fargo, and the others knew the postmaster general was a southerner, and they went along. But not you."

"Even Butterfield made a mistake," Merle said, on the defensive. "His original route was six hundred miles north of this one."

"But he changed it. You didn't."

Merle knew she was right. He had not thought a southern route feasible. Even now, with the Apaches out of control, he was sure he was right. For a time he had the Northern press on his side. They dubbed the route the "oxbow," a term of derision based on the route's U shape, which they argued took the least-direct route west. Most of the newspapers predicted that the venture would be a total failure. Yet since the contract with Butterfield had taken effect, the route had proven to be the best choice. Grass and water were available for the livestock, and the road could be driven all year long. There were four other routes operating now, but the Butterfield coaches were the only ones that consistently got through with the mail—generally in twenty-five days or less. This was a bitter pill for Jenkins to swallow. He had spent so much time trying to discredit Butterfield and the route that he had lost out on bids for these other routes.

"No use quarreling about it now," said Cornwallis, opening the door on the side where Stack had gotten out. "But I do believe, Merle, that your Apaches have gotten out of hand."

"They were not supposed to attack this far west," said Jenkins. "I wonder if they found the rifles."

Cornwallis coughed and got out. That was a question he did not want Merle to pursue. The congressman knew it was possible that Mangas had been infuriated upon finding the old muzzle-loading Enfields and had gone on a killing rampage. The only satisfaction he had now was in knowing the stage had been allowed to come so far already without being harmed.

Anne Jenkins continued to fan herself after alighting from the stage. She and her husband, with Cornwallis trailing them, walked some distance from the stage to get away from the smell of burnt wood and flesh. Still angry, she stopped and continued her tirade.

"You have blood on your hands, Merle, and the Lord will exact payment."

"The Apaches were only supposed to run off the stationmen," he said feebly. "Not kill them."

"The blood is on your head." A crazy look came into the woman's eyes—a look that told Merle she was on the verge of hysteria.

"Keep your voice down," he warned.

"I think your wife is ill from the heat," ventured the congressman. "The body loses salts—"

"I am not ill, Hiram! I am frightened. Frightened out

of my wits. When you make a pact with the Devil, then you put yourself on his level. The both of you are responsible for this senseless slaughter! No good can come of it! I wouldn't be surprised if the government shut down all stage routes on account of you two! Who will want to ride in our coaches with bloodthirsty Indians waiting behind every rock?''

-''Now, now, Anne, calm down,'' soothed Merle. ''This will all blow over. With Hiram's help, we can obtain a contract. By then the Indians will have been contained, I'm sure.''

''You're sure? You're insane, Merle! You can't stop this! It's too late!'' Anne broke down then, weeping hysterically. Merle put his arms around her shoulders, but she pushed him away, sobbing so violently that the sounds carried to Morty and the two men with him.

''Make her be quiet,'' commanded Cornwallis. ''That damned driver is coming this way.''

Anne screamed then, her fury spilling over the banks of reason in a flood tide of anguish.

That's when Merle hit her, hard. Anne swooned in his arms.

''What's the trouble here?'' asked a breathless Morty.

''Nothing,'' said Cornwallis calmly. ''Everything's under control. I suggest you get the coach moving. This is no place to linger. This poor woman has fainted from the sight of this slaughter.''

Stuart Gorman came running up and was stopped by the glare of hatred in Cornwallis's eyes.

Stuart helped Merle carry his wife back to the coach. He dreaded being alone with the congressman. That look had told him a great deal. There had been murder in Cornwallis's eyes—pure murder.

The dead horse was still warm.

Luke Faraday slid his hand from its underside, as Lorene looked on from the saddle of her horse.

''What happened?'' she asked.

''Horse broke its leg. One of Bodine's men had to

shoot it.'' The saddle lay in the sun, a lizard peeping out from under it.

Luke scanned the ground, reading the signs. "They've got two horses packing double," he said. "Bodine won't like that much. It slows him down and wears out the animals."

Lorene raised a hand to her mouth. "That means Chastity . . ." She couldn't finish what was on her mind.

"He won't kill her," said Luke, trying to soften the blow. "He needs her to get Vernon Blaine to let Morgan out."

"If . . . if . . ."

Luke strode back to his horse. "Look," he said quietly, "don't try to figure out what might happen. The girl is alive. We'll catch up to them tonight or tomorrow."

"And then what?"

"Then you can worry."

The sun splashed a lusty blood-red stain over the sky beyond Apache Pass. The desert colors softened, the shadows deepened.

Luke Faraday pulled his horse to an abrupt halt.

"Why are we stopping?" Lorene asked. She felt fit and exhilarated. Once, from a hill, they had spotted Bodine, still riding Luke's stolen gelding. And Lorene was positive she had seen the distinctive cloth of Chastity's dress. She had thought them near, but Luke had explained that distances were deceptive in the clear air and that Bodine was at least two hours ahead if they rode hard. It was a disappointment, but now she was eager to go on. All the time they had been riding, she had felt close to Chastity. In her mind, Chastity was just over the next rise. But the miles had stretched on until the sun had escaped with its light.

"If Bodine goes through the pass now, he's got five miles of darkness to get out of it. The pass is narrow and stacked high with rocks—good hiding places for any Apache worth his salt. If my hunch is still working, I'd say

Mangas is in there right now, just waiting for someone to ride through.''

"But, Bodine . . ."

"If he's smart, he'll wait until it's dark and then try to sneak through. And he *is* smart. I tracked him many a mile, and he didn't make many mistakes.''

"Are we just going to wait here?''

"For Morty's stage. It will make our chances much better to go through together. I've seen their dust trail all afternoon, and they're not far behind. If I know Morty, he's planning to take the pass after dark, too.''

As if his words were a command, Lorene turned and saw the dust trail rising in the air. Soon the stage rumbled up, a dirty, begrimed Morty Tubbs slapping reins and spitting tobacco juice into the air.

"Whoaaaa!" yelled Morty, setting the brake.

The Concord, all twenty-five hundred pounds of it, rumbled to a stop, its bright green paint glistening in the last rays of the sun. The body rocked on its leather thoroughbraces, the straps creaking under the strain. Normally, such coaches were used only at the beginning and end of each journey, smaller and simpler wagons being used over the rough roads in between. But this was not the regular coach—it was John Butterfield's personal stage. And it was plain that Morty had enjoyed his ride. He grinned when he saw Luke and Lorene. So did Stuart, seated next to him.

"Catch up to Bodine yet?''

"He's at the mouth of the pass, likely,'' Luke replied. "Best get some grub out if you can spare it.''

Morty wrapped the reins around the brake. "You figger to take the pass after dark?''

"Quiet and slow,'' Luke answered.

Supper was bacon, beans, bread, and onions—all cold. Anne Jenkins couldn't eat. She sat morosely silent.

After supper, Luke told them his plan. "Once Bodine gets into the pass, he can't come back. If Apaches are in there, he'll draw their fire. We have a chance to get through while he keeps them busy, and hopefully rescue Chastity in the process.''

"I don't think the Apaches will attack the coach,'' Jenkins said boldly.

Cornwallis skewered him with a reprimanding look.

Luke missed the exchange, but Stuart didn't. Neither did Stack. They looked at Jenkins oddly, puzzled.

"Prime your weapons,'' Luke continued. "Soon as the last light goes, we'll leave.''

Luke and Lorene left to tend to their horses. Morty and Stuart began checking the stagecoach, looking at the broad iron tires that would not sink in mud and were set five feet two inches apart to keep the coach from tipping.

"Merle, I want to talk to you,'' Cornwallis said in a low whisper. Looking at Anne, he added, "Alone.''

The two men walked some distance away from the campfire.

"What is it, Hiram?''

"I'm going to kill Gorman tonight.''

"What? You can't be serious. You'll be seen. We'll—''

"Shut up and listen. There won't be any deal for you if he lives. And you have to do your part, too.''

"What's that?''

"Shoot that woman—Lorene Martin. Those are the only two who know about me. Dammit, Merle, just do it. I've got to get those papers out of her saddlebag. Well?''

"I'll try. When?''

"When the shooting starts up in the pass. And don't count on those Apaches not attacking the coach. Just use it to your advantage.''

"What do you mean? About the Apaches . . . ?''

Cornwallis didn't have to answer. The darkness had settled, and the first sounds of gunfire crackled in the distance—a lone shot, followed by a deafening volley.

"Come on!'' yelled Luke, swinging into the saddle. "Morty, move 'em out! Lorene and I will bring up the rear.''

As the passengers scrambled into the coach, Morty leaped up onto the driver's seat. Stuart was already there, with a rifle ready in his hands. The driver unwrapped the reins from the brake, released it, and reached for his whip. With a mighty crack, the whip snapped over the heads of the horses. The Concord lurched and began rolling. Stack and the others slammed the doors and took up rifles in readiness.

Ahead, high in the pass, muzzle flashes sparkled, twinkling like fireflies. The reports followed, sounding like firecrackers at a Chinese party.

Close in, savage shouts and screams carried on the air. The stage, rocking in its thoroughbraces, raced up toward the narrow pass—the one called Doubtful by those who knew its treachery.

Morty cracked the whip and yelled over the noise of the team as if driving straight into hell. As they shot into the pass, he dropped the whip and picked up the Greener shotgun. He cocked both barrels with his thumb.

There was no stopping now. No going back.

Chapter 10

Deep in Apache Pass, the first rifle shot froze Ernie Bodine and his men in their tracks. It had been fired from somewhere above them, but no muzzle flash had been seen in the darkness.

Will Peeker was the first to crack. He drew his pistol and fired in the direction of the shot, shooting as fast as he could hammer back and pull the trigger, until his revolver was empty.

"You bastard!" Bodine cursed at him. "What in hell you shootin' at? Ain't seen no flash!"

As Peeker scrambled to reload, Bodine looked around, trying to make out the surroundings in the thin moonlight. Their three remaining horses were strung in a line, with the four outlaws walking beside them. The horses' hooves were wrapped in cloth torn from shirttails and the bottom of Chastity Blaine's dress, in an attempt to muffle the iron shoes. Chastity was seated on Bodine's mount, her wrists lashed together to the saddle horn. It was a cruel act on Bodine's part, but he figured she would serve to draw the Indians' fire, if necessary.

It was quiet again, with the eerie stillness that settles just after dusk and before the nighthawks begin to knife the air. Still, it was strange not to hear the drum of a prairie chicken or the plaintive yodel of a coyote—as if nature was holding its breath.

Bodine began to walk his mount slowly, stopping to listen every so often. Suddenly, other rifles opened up from the rocks behind them. Rafe Adams, bringing up the rear, whirled and fired his pistol at one of the orange flashes.

"They're behind us!" whispered Dan Rawlings.

"Shut up!" growled Bodine. "Save your ammunition. They want us to shoot back so they can see where we are!"

The others, seeing the sense in what he said, held their fire. The rocks were only shadows, and the firing from them was sporadic, the aim poor. Here, deep on the floor of the pass, the outlaws and their horses were practically invisible. Only Chastity's dress showed in the darkness.

Bodine moved ahead, knowing their retreat was blocked. He hugged the rocks on one side, presenting as poor a target as possible as he hunched low near the horse's forelegs. It was Chastity, he realized, who presented the best target, lashed to the saddle. If they got close enough to see her and fired, he'd have a chance.

He could always find another way to break Chet Morgan out of prison.

Mangas Sangrías, from his position high in the pass, listened to the shooting and smiled thinly in the dark.

He had placed warriors all along the narrow pass, making sure they were well hidden in the rocks. Many of them did not have rifles. Only a very few had pistols, and these were single-shot. But they had lances, bows, arrows, and the new Enfield rifles, which Mangas had given to only the hardiest of his band, men who were stationed deeper in the pass, their rifles fixed on strategic points. Some of the warriors would be mobile, harassing and harrying the white eyes on through the pass. Those who were firing now were told only to block any escape to the rear. From the sounds, these warriors were doing their jobs well.

Mangas was a bitter man. He had reason to be bitter. Once he had trusted, or at least tolerated, the white eyes—as had his chief, Juan José Compá. In those days, the Mexicans in Sonora rose up against the Indians and began offering a one-hundred-peso bounty for the scalps of Apache braves. Then they began offering bounties of fifty pesos for women's scalps and twenty-five pesos for those of children. Infuriated, Apache bands raided the Mexicans with renewed fury.

It was in the white man's year of 1837 that an Anglo bounty hunter named James Johnson, who had gained the friendship of Compá, made a secret contract with the governor of Sonora. He lured Juan José and his band to a fiesta in the Sierra de las Ánimas. Johnson had a cannon hidden from view, and while several hundred of the Apache were all packed together at the feast, the cannon was fired into their midst. Many Indians were killed and wounded. All of them were confused. Taking advantage of their bewilderment, Johnson and his men attacked, killing Apaches with guns, knives, and clubs. Johnson personally killed his former friend, Juan José. Mangas had been a witness to this betrayal and slaughter, and this was the act that hardened him into a bitter enemy of all Anglos.

Mangas was a shrewd planner, a man who knew how to exploit an enemy's weakness. Following the massacre of his chief and friends, he had reunited and armed several scattered Apache bands and had led them against the Anglo trappers, miners, and settlers, and finally against the army of the bluecoats itself.

Now he was determined to wipe out these whites in the pass. One had lied to him, and the others would die as well. Warriors were waiting next to bundles of dry brush lashed together. Once the majority of the white eyes were in the pass, with their retreat cut off, the brush would be fired and thrown down from the rocks. The Indians would be in darkness. The white eyes would be visible in the firelight—easy targets.

Mangas gave an order, which was carried along the

pass. At once, the shooting died down and Mangas waited. The Apaches grew quiet in the rocks, listening.

Bodine wondered why there was no more shooting.

Chastity, frightened first by the disembodied rifle shots and now by the dark silence, grew frantic at her predicament. She began working to free herself, tugging on her bonds. The leather thongs cut into her wrists, but she felt them stretch. Forcing herself to ignore the pain, she lifted her body and put all her weight on the thongs lashed to the saddle horn. Little by little, the lashings loosened.

Bodine heard a stagecoach coming. Now he knew why the Apaches had stopped firing.

He jerked on the reins, pulling the horse along behind him. He moved faster, hoping he could get through. Perhaps the Apaches were only after the stage. At any rate, none of his bunch had been shot. Rawlings caught up with him a few moments later, with Peeker hanging on to the horse's tail.

"Awful quiet," Rawlings said.

"We ain't out of it yet," said Bodine.

Rafe Adams came upon them shortly after, as puzzled as they.

"Don't bunch up," said Bodine. "Stay to the deep shadows and don't talk no more!"

He led the way as the pounding hooves of the stage came closer. Less than a mile, he figured, until the stage was in the pass to stay.

Bodine hurried, but he knew the calm was too good to last. The pass was five miles long, and if Mangas wanted to, he could attack at any point along its length.

Morty Tubbs also wondered why the shooting had stopped. He drove the stage team hard into the pass, hunching low in the driver's seat. Stuart Gorman looked up at the black rocks—shapeless monsters looming over them—and he wondered if his life would explode into blackness once the shooting started again. His throat was clogged with a lump he could not swallow. Sweat slicked his hands on the rifle. And he realized, with shame, that his knees were knocking, not from the motion of the coach, but from a fearful shaking inside him that he could not control.

Luke Faraday held his horse back, both to avoid the choking dust and to watch for any Apaches jumping down from the rocks to attack the stage. Lorene rode beside him, leaning over her horse's neck as if she were doing the jumps in a steeplechase.

Morty guided the stage by instinct and memory, keeping the horses from crashing into the steep banks of the pass, then easing them into a slower gait when they began to get out of control.

Suddenly the shooting resumed, this time from somewhere in the rocks behind the stage.

Morty heard a lead ball thunk into the back of his seat and yelled at Stuart, "Hang on, young feller! We're gonna be buried up to the hub nuts in Apaches!"

Luke heard the balls whine through the air and carom off the rocks. He twisted in the saddle and saw the orange flash. An arrow sailed close by, its sound a low *whoooosh*. The flint head struck stone, giving off a shower of sparks.

"Ride on, Lorene!" he yelled. "Stay inside the dust of the coach!"

She nodded as she rode by, unable to speak, the wind in her teeth, the dust a gritty and blinding cloud that choked her lungs. The sound of rifle fire and the sizzle of balls sent shivers up her spine. She saw no Apaches and was grateful. The fear in her heart was a clutching hand, with steely fingers tightening on her windpipe.

Luke slowed, trying to determine a pattern to the attack.

Just then the firing stopped as abruptly as it had begun. There were no visible targets. All Luke could make out in the darkness was the stage as it rumbled through the pass, with Lorene swept up in its boiling wake.

Then it struck him. The Apaches wanted them to go on. Not through, but deeper into the pass. Ahead, he was sure, Mangas was waiting with the main body of his band, ready to slaughter them like fish in a rain barrel.

Faraday savagely dug in his spurs and whacked his horse's rump. Somehow, he had to get ahead of the stage and warn them!

Even as his horse's hind legs dug in and the animal spurted ahead, Luke saw a bush or something burst into flames two or three hundred yards ahead. And then he heard the hoarse yells of men, followed by the boom of big-caliber rifles.

Mangas gave the signal and warriors hunched over tinder and struck flints to stone. Sparks flew. Braves sprawled on their bellies and blew on the sparks. The first bundle of brush exploded into flame. With a mighty yell, two braves kicked the blazing bundle from the rocks and watched it roll down, sparking and flaming, onto the narrow road below.

Bodine saw the bundle topple. In the glow of its wake, he saw the silhouetted shapes of half-naked warriors yelling a battle cry. He fired and saw a dark shape throw up its arms and topple from the rocks. Peeker yelled and began firing his pistol.

More brush blazed. Shots sounded in the boulders. Lead balls seared the air, ricocheting with angry whines.

Bodine dropped to the ground and began searching for a target for his rifle as he reloaded quickly, pouring powder down the barrel, seating the ball, setting the percussion cap in place. He saw an Apache stand up to reload, aimed for his chest, and fired. The Apache died with a bloodcurdling scream, falling head over heels into the road. Indian rifles found his position and fired. Lead balls kicked dust and grit into his face. He rolled, still holding his empty rifle as he drew his pistol with his other hand.

Bodine saw his horse break away, but Chastity was no longer seated upon it. In the confusion, he had forgotten all about her. Now it appeared she had escaped, or perhaps had been shot. His eyes searched for her light dress, but he saw nothing.

The stage was still approaching, and Apaches were now leaping from the cliff in bunches. Rafe Adams mounted his horse as a band of Apaches jumped down from the opposite side, yelling war cries with strident, excited voices.

Bodine scrambled on all fours, scuttling after his horse, which had come to a halt nearby. He grabbed the reins, lifted his pistol, and shot an Apache point-blank in the face as the warrior came up out of the dark, brandishing a war club. Bodine holstered his pistol, stuck a foot in the stirrup, and grabbed the saddle horn with one hand, his empty rifle still in the other. He climbed up, rammed the rifle in its scabbard, and spurred the horse forward.

Chastity was hiding in the rocks beside the road. She had leaped from Bodine's horse as soon as she had worked her hands loose from the saddle horn. Now she fought the leather thongs with her teeth, finally freeing her wrists.

As she tossed the thongs to the dirt, she saw the stagecoach come barreling by. She screamed, but her shout was swallowed up by the noise of gunfire, screaming Apaches, horses, and white men yelling. Ahead, she saw Rafe Adams ride into a group of Apaches. A second later, he was jerked from his horse, and a knife flashed up and down in the moonlight. Fire bundles lit the road, and she saw dozens of dark, half-naked shapes dash by, chasing after Bodine.

Rafe screamed once before his throat was slashed from ear to ear.

Peeker materialized out of the dust and grabbed up the reins of Rafe's horse. As he mounted he fired two quick shots, dropping two Apaches. He rode off as Bodine wheeled his own horse.

Bodine yelled at Rawlings to get mounted. Rawlings took a running jump and landed in the saddle of his spooked horse. An Apache on the rocks took aim with a big Enfield. Rawlings took the bullet in his side, wobbled, and kept going as Peeker and Bodine covered him with pistol fire.

Apaches leaped down beyond Bodine, blocking the road through the pass. Peeker yelled and charged forward,

a second pistol in his hand. Bodine whirled his horse and
rode into the Indians, shooting over his horse's head.
Apaches screamed, scrambling out of the way as rifle fire
bloomed on the hillside like bright orange flowers. But the
outlaws rode on, leaving the ambush behind as they raced
toward the lowland beyond.

Back in the pass, the stagecoach ground over a dead
Apache, tossing the passengers out of their seats. The
stage shuddered to a halt as the dead man's body acted as a
brake on the rear wheel.

Lieutenant Stack was shooting out one window. Merle
Jenkins picked himself up and tried to get back to the other
window. Cornwallis shoved him aside. Then the congressman took deliberate aim at the roof of the coach. The
angle he chose would take a bullet straight into Gorman's
body if he was still riding shotgun. He fired, and smoke
filled the coach.

Stack turned around, staring at Cornwallis, who was
framed by firelight. "What the hell are you doing?"

"Pistol just went off," Cornwallis said lamely, hoping Stack would believe him.

Jenkins, shaking and out of breath, struggled to his
seat.

Anne Jenkins, numb with shock and fear, huddled in
the corner. But that didn't save her. An Apache rose up
out of nowhere, his moccasined feet on the running board
as he aimed a bow and arrow through the window. Anne
screamed as the Apache fired. The arrow twanged into her
chest. She slumped over, then tumbled to the floor of the
coach.

Stuart Gorman had felt the congressman's shot thunk
into the back of his seat. He whirled and saw the Apache
shoot the arrow inside the coach. He leaned over, shooting
straight at the broadest part of the Indian's back. The brave
fell with a thud.

"Got him!" Stuart yelled, more amazed than proud.
But now he began picking out targets, firing his pistol at
every brave within range until it was empty.

Morty cracked the reins, yelling at the horses in an effort to get the stage moving again.

Lorene rode up to the stalled coach, reached down, and jerked free the dead brave who was blocking the wheel.

"You can move now!" she called. Her face was smeared with burnt powder, chalked with dust. She trotted up beside the window.

Jenkins heard her and leaned out the window, his pistol cocked. Lorene looked at him, horrified. Jenkins took aim. Lorene ducked, and he squeezed the trigger.

The ball whistled over Lorene's head. She rose up, glared at the dismayed Jenkins, and kicked her horse. The animal bolted past a pair of Apaches, who tried to pull her from the horse. Morty fired both barrels of his Greener, and the Apaches twitched as buckshot struck their backs. Then they fell, mortally wounded.

Luke saw Chastity hiding in the rocks. Nearby, an Apache was crawling toward her like a lizard, his body gleaming bronze in the firelight. The sounds of shooting had dwindled as men poured powder down barrels and rammed lead balls on top.

Chastity heard a sound behind her and twisted to look up. The Apache leaped.

Luke hammered back and fired his Colt .44. The Apache twisted in midair, his face contorted in pain. Chastity leaped from her hiding place and ran down the road in terror as the Apache hit the rocks with a crunch and rolled down the face of a boulder like a broken rag doll.

As Chastity appeared in the moonlight, Indian rifle fire sought her out. Luke saw her danger and kicked his horse into action. He rode by, leaned over, and snaked an arm around her waist, swooping her up onto his lap as he slid back in the saddle.

Nearby, the stage rumbled forward, freed of the dead Apache. Morty Tubbs wrestled the team back on course as balls ripped into the luggage and whistled past his ears. Lorene, hugging her saddle, shot an Apache as he tried to leap onto the stage. He took the ball in the throat as his hands touched the rail, gripped it for a second, then slid off. His body hit the ground and skidded along the road.

Sporadic rifle fire followed the stage and the horses bearing Lorene, Luke, and Chastity as they barreled through the pass. High above them, Mangas rose up from his hiding place, his barrel smoking.

Several braves started to run for their horses. "Wait!" he said loudly.

Corto halted the others. "We can catch them," he argued. "We can bring back many white scalps."

The firelight flickered along the road. Mangas's painted face danced with shadows, the colors seeming to run together, separating and reforming in grotesque patterns. The lines of age etched into his face seemed to deepen, harden.

"Pick up our dead, Corto. We have done enough fighting this night. Without repeating rifles or the pistols that shoot six times, we cannot win."

"We have pistols now, from one of the white eyes down there." Corto shook Rafe's bloody scalp. Another brave brandished two pistols and a powder horn.

"Two pistols, when we need fifty," Mangas shrugged.

"We will get more," Corto insisted. "We will get the rifles that shoot many times, too."

Mangas sighed. His men were flushed with the hot blood that rushes through a man during a fight. But he was old and tired. One scalp for the spirits of several good men did not seem worth the effort.

"There are no such repeating rifles, Corto."

"Yes. I have seen them."

"Only pistols with rifle stocks. Those are no good. They do not shoot well, and they jam."

"Jenkins said the repeaters were real rifles."

Mangas waved Corto away. The white eyes had strong medicine, and he was getting old. There were too many changes. Even the ponies did not seem so fast anymore. And there were fewer and fewer braves willing to stand up and fight. More and more bluecoats were coming into the country, using Apache scouts to uncover all the good

Indian hiding places. The big land was suddenly smaller, and there was little game to hunt.

Slowly, dreamily, Mangas began to reload his rifle. It was only a habit. He had little fight left in him. Just anger. And even that wasn't enough to make his heart strong again.

Apache Pass dropped down onto monotonous plains fringed with high hills, faintly visible in the glow of the moon. As the stagecoach clattered out across the valley, Morty Tubbs hauled back on the reins, touching the brake.

"Whoa!" he called.

Lorene halted, Luke and Chastity right behind her.

The horses pulling the stage were blowing hard. "Nigh run 'em into the ground," wheezed Morty, setting the brake. "Got to let 'em blow or they'll founder for sure."

Luke let Chastity down gently. "Are you all right?" he asked.

She gasped and nodded.

"I'll keep a lookout," said Faraday. "We hit them hard, but there could be a few diehards chasing us."

Lorene's side ached, but she said nothing. She rode over to Luke, wondering whether to tell him about Jenkins shooting at her. Not now. Not with danger so close and so many other things crowding her mind. The ride through the pass had been like a dream—a nightmare. The screaming Apaches, the rifle fire, the dead men going down. She almost wanted to pinch herself to make sure she was not dreaming. But the smell of burnt powder in her nostrils told her that all of it had been real.

Luke looked at her, trying to imagine the rich copper of her hair, the sparkle in her eyes. He saw only shadows where her eyes were—the dark outline of her nose and lips.

"You did well," he said softly.

There was a commotion inside the stage. "Help me!" someone shouted. "My wife—she's been shot!"

Merle Jenkins was holding the door open. Someone inside the coach was trying to light the lantern.

Luke jumped down from his horse. He looked inside the coach. Stack was holding Anne's head in his lap. Cornwallis lit another sulphur match. The flame sputtered, the wick glowed orange and blue. At last the oil burned and light glimmered inside the Concord. Jenkins held the door open as Luke slid in and looked at the arrow jutting from Anne's breast.

He cursed silently. Anne's eyes were closed. Blood flecked her lips. Her face was bone white, the lips blue.

"I'll have to get the arrow out," said Faraday. "Cornwallis, you got any spirits?"

"Eh?"

"Whiskey? Brandy? She may need some. And get something for her to bite on. Lieutenant, you hold her real steady."

Jenkins wadded up a fresh handkerchief and gave it to Faraday, who opened her mouth and stuffed it between her teeth. He'd seen people bite through their lips under such an ordeal. Cornwallis knew better than to offer his water-filled flask, so he reached under the seat for his carry bag and produced a bottle of whiskey, which he held to Anne's quivering lips. Morty and Gorman stood outside, peering through the window. Chastity stood near Merle Jenkins, holding on to the same door. Lorene remained on her horse, nervously watching the trail leading down from the pass.

"Hold on, ma'am," Luke said quietly. "This is going to hurt some."

He wiped his palms, snapped the feathered end off the arrow, and took the remaining shaft in both hands, holding it steady so it would not rip any bigger hole coming out the other side. The arrow had struck her just above her right breast—far from the heart, but probably puncturing a lung. Gritting his teeth, Luke rose up and pushed hard, putting all of his weight on his arms and wrists. Anne's eyes came open. The arrowhead slid through, coming out her back.

Her muffled scream was weak. Tears drenched her face. Quickly, Luke turned her over slightly until he could reach the arrowhead and the bloody shaft. He grasped the slick shaft with both hands and pulled. The rest of the arrow came through, but Anne began shaking with convulsions.

He rolled her over on her back again, threw the arrow down, and reached for the flask in Cornwallis's trembling hand. Then he paused and turned to the door.

"Jenkins," he said, "you'd better get in here and say good-bye to her."

Anne's eyes frosted over with the glaze of death. She moaned. Luke moved out of the way as Jenkins scrambled inside and took his wife's hand. She seemed to stare right through him, then she shuddered once and closed her eyes.

Jenkins began sobbing. Luke got out of the coach and drew a deep breath.

"Is she—did she . . . ?" Lorene stammered.

"Yes," he said. "She's gone."

Jenkins sobbed loudly, then began ranting. "It—it's all my fault, Anne. I'm so sorry! Please don't leave me! Anne? Anne, you can't die."

Morty opened the coach door. "We'll have to put her on top," he said, his tone kindly. "Mr. Jenkins, we're all sorry. I'll need help. Lieutenant, Stuart, give me a hand. We'll be real gentle with her, Mr. Jenkins."

Jenkins looked at Tubbs with red-rimmed eyes. "You fool! You can't put her up there! They'll get her, mutilate her."

"Calm down, man," said Cornwallis. "She'll be safe."

"We'll bury her at the next way station—Dragoon Springs," said Morty. "Better than out here."

Jenkins began sobbing again, and Luke had to pry his hand loose from his wife's. He helped the man over to the side of the road and hunched down with him.

"I'm sorry," said Jenkins. "I didn't mean to do it. Any of it. Anne, can you ever forgive me?"

Luke looked at him, wondering what kind of troubles the man had that none of them knew about. "You have to live with it, Jenkins," he said.

Lorene, nearby, bit her lip. This was not the time to say anything about him shooting at her. Jenkins was grief stricken. His sobbing wrenched at her senses. The man had a lot to answer for, and perhaps in time he would. Already, it seemed, he was paying a high price for his deeds.

She turned away and saw Cornwallis in the coach, staring at her. His face seemed etched out of granite—cold, forbidding, full of hate. She shuddered, suddenly chill.

Chapter 11

They wrapped the body of Anne Jenkins in a blanket and strapped her to the top of the stage. Gorman, Stack, and Tubbs did it all while Cornwallis brooded in the coach and Jenkins got his emotions under control. Lorene comforted Chastity, helping her change into fresh clothes behind a stunted clump of trees.

Stuart was about to climb down from the stage when Stack put a hand on his arm. "Cornwallis got anything against you, son?"

"I—I suppose so. I—I can't talk about it."

"Well, you better look inside that coach."

"What're you drivin' at?" asked Tubbs.

"Might have been accidental," said the lieutenant, "but there's a bullet hole in the roof, and I'd swear that ball was meant for you. I didn't see him shoot, but during the fighting his pistol went off, and it stamped a hole right behind your back, Gorman. Of course he says it was an accident."

Stuart went pale. He climbed down, stepped inside the coach, and saw the ragged hole. He touched it with his finger.

Cornwallis glared at him.

"Did you try to shoot me, Mr. Cornwallis?"

"I don't know what you're talking about, son. I just

know you'll never work in Washington again. Or anywhere else, if I can help it."

"You—you, charlatan!" Stuart blurted, reaching for the congressman's collar.

Cornwallis squirmed away, but Gorman grasped the lapels of his coat and started shaking him. Cornwallis yelled for help as he tried to slide across the seat, but Stuart would not release his grip. He shoved and shook the politician until Cornwallis's teeth rattled.

Luke left Jenkins and went to see what was going on. Lorene and Chastity got back to the coach just as Luke started to pull Stuart off Cornwallis.

"He tried to shoot me!" said Gorman. "He tried to kill me!"

"The boy is lying!" said the ruffled Cornwallis. "Get him out of here!"

"Look!" said Stuart, pointing to the bullet hole. Quickly, he told Luke what Stack had said.

Lorene heard it all. "Jenkins tried to kill me," she added. "He shot at me and just barely missed."

"I ought to put you both afoot," Faraday said. "But instead, I'm going to ask for your arms. If you don't surrender them, I'll slug you both and tie you up in the boot."

Meekly, Cornwallis surrendered his pistol and rifle. Jenkins did the same.

"Lieutenant," Luke told Stack, "you keep an eye on these two. Any trouble, shoot 'em."

"Be happy to," said Stack, glad to have some responsibility.

"Morty, get this stage rolling and don't stop until you get to Dragoon Springs. Chastity, climb up into the coach. Gorman, are you able to ride shotgun without letting your temper get away from you again?"

"Yes, sir," said the youth.

"Then get up there and keep looking over your shoulder. Lorene, if you're still with me, let's ride ahead. I think one of Bodine's men is wounded. He'll be slowed down, and we might catch him if we press him hard."

"Lead on, Mr. Faraday," she said, and he could almost see her brave smile in the dark—could almost feel her weariness, her sadness at having taken a human life.

As the moon began to rise over Yuma Prison that same Tuesday night, Chet Morgan ran his hand across the pistol barrel. The bluing was worn, but the action was true and tight. Each of the other men had pistols, too. It had taken some doing—some money, some promises. Morgan had arranged for an outside accomplice to smuggle the weapons into the prison concealed in butchered hogs' bellies. The cooks had transferred them to one of the prisoners, Jorge Mendoza, one night when he sang for the guards at dinner. When he packed his guitar, the pistols were put inside before he closed the case. Neat, slick.

Then Jorge had passed them along, wrapped in long cloth strips and swung from cell to cell through the windows on the outside walls. Powder, ball, and percussion caps had been transferred the same way.

Now, as Morgan waited for the evening meal to be brought down to the cells, he mentally practiced his moves. Arneson had played sick all day, so that when the chow wagon reached him, the guards would have to open his cell door to give him his tray. Arneson was the coolest of the bunch that was breaking out. He'd surprise them with his revolver and force them to release Chet Morgan, Jorge Mendoza, and another prisoner, Wade Denton. It would be quick, Morgan hoped. The guards were not armed in this part of the prison, but there might be blood spilled when the escapees made their way to Vernon Blaine's quarters.

Morgan heard the iron door open at the end of the hall, followed by the clatter of the food cart. Small trapdoors opened at each cell as trays of beans and bacon were shoved in onto the dirt floors.

Morgan got up and shoved the pistol inside his loose prison shirt, holding on to the butt. He leaned against the wall next to Arneson's cell, listening.

"Get up, Arneson," said the guard.

No answer.

"Better take a look, Bob."

"Hell, he ain't movin'."

"Maybe he's dead. Open it up."

Morgan sucked in his breath and held it. Keys rattled, the lock clanged, the door slid open. Footsteps padded on the cell floor.

"Hey, Arneson, you—"

"Bob, just hold steady," Arneson coolly demanded, leveling his pistol at them. "Jim, you step inside the cell. Make one sound and I'll kill you."

Jim entered the cell, and Arneson took the keys from him. "Turn and face the wall," he said.

Morgan counted the long seconds. Then he heard a sharp crack and a moan, followed by a thud.

"Hey, Arneson . . ." protested Jim. And then he, too, was slugged to the floor, unconscious.

Arnie ran to Morgan's cell and opened it nervously. Morgan was ready.

"Get Jorge and Wade out," he said tightly, running to the main door at the end of the hall. The guards had carelessly left it open. The other prisoners watched—they were short-termers who had decided against escape. Morgan paid them no attention.

When the three others were with him, he stepped into the main hall. There were four more guards to take care of before they reached Blaine's quarters. They caught them all by surprise, using their pistols as clubs and knocking them unconscious. One, who resisted more than the others, tried to run. Jorge hit him hard, again and again, until the man's skull was pulp. Arneson pulled the Mexican off. Jorge's eyes glittered, and there was spittle at the corners of his mouth.

Morgan put his shoulder to the door leading to the warden's quarters and forced it open. Blaine was lying down, a magazine tented on his chest. He rose up, his mouth open, and Morgan shoved the barrel of the pistol into his mouth.

"One sound, Blaine, and you're wolf meat."

Blaine gagged. Arneson jerked him to his feet. Morgan moved around Blaine and rammed the barrel into his back.

"Move!"

Blaine stumbled through the door, bullied by the four men.

"You'll never make it, Morgan," hissed Blaine. Wade Denton rammed a knee into Blaine's groin. The warden paled and doubled over.

"Easy," said Morgan. "We want him able to walk across the yard."

The guards outside along the wall saw the men coming. As they raised their rifles, Denton, Jorge, and Arnie opened fire. The guards ducked, tried to take aim, but on Blaine's order were forced to drop their rifles. Arnie fumbled with the keys and opened the gate. The three convicts, pushing the warden in front of them, raced through and down the hill to where their outside accomplice waited with horses.

One of the guards picked up his rifle and crawled to the other side of the wall. He picked out a running man and fired.

Jorge took the slug in the back. His footsteps faltered as a red stain spread across his back. He went down, gasping for air. Morgan turned and fired two shots at the guard.

Wade stopped to help the Mexican. "Leave him," said Morgan. "We ain't got time to dally." He shoved Blaine forward.

The outside man, Zeke Stokes, waited nervously behind a small adobe shack. Stokes lived just outside the prison, where he raised pork and cattle, which he sold to the warden. But it was hard, brutal work with little return. Morgan had promised him a cut in the payroll money if he helped them escape.

"Stokes, you did right well," Morgan said. "Coming along? Jorge didn't make it. That's more for the rest of us."

"Hell, I can't stay here. They'll put two and two together." Stokes was a burly man, his face deeply tanned from the sun. He had no family, and he liked money.

"You're a scoundrel, Stokes," muttered Blaine. "We trusted you."

"Shut up, Blaine," said Morgan. "Tie his hands and get him on a horse," he said to Wade.

The men panted, out of breath, but there was no time to waste. It wouldn't take long for a posse to be raised. They mounted up. Morgan patted his saddlebags and jiggled his canteens. Stokes had thought of everything. The horses were sound, with rifles snugged in the saddle scabbards.

"Where to?" asked Arnie.

"We'll stay on the stage road and intercept the coach east of Maricopa Wells. If Bodine's on it, we'll get him off."

"Might have the army with him," said Stokes.

"They won't be no trouble. I know a place not far beyond Maricopa—a Pima Indian village. Stage always stops there to give the folks a look at wild Indians." Morgan laughed. "That's where we'll take it."

"Why not go straight to your payroll cache?" asked Arneson.

Morgan gave him a sharp look. "In time, Arnie, in time. With Bodine coming we can get his half, too, and there'll be a lot more money to go around. Savvy?"

He took up the reins of Vernon Blaine's horse. "Let's ride," he said, kneeing his mount. The horse, a deep chestnut, bounded away. Morgan's lips curled back as he tasted the sweet air of freedom.

Lorene had trouble keeping up with Luke Faraday after they left Dragoon Springs in the small hours of the morning. The station, at least, was intact, and they had been able to exchange horses. But there had been no word of Apaches or Bodine. Yet Luke had later found a sign that Bodine had passed by when he picked up a bloody rag that caught his eye. He sniffed it and felt the blood. It had dried, but it was fairly fresh. Under a lighted match, the blood was red and had not faded much.

They grabbed snatches of sleep when they could,

knowing Bodine and his men would have to do the same.
From Dragoon Springs, the road led through deep gullies
and over dry creek beds. At times, they rode across an-
cient walls, finally reaching an endless stretch of mesquite
timber—stunted trees thickly dotting the land.

A few hours beyond Dragoon Springs, they crossed
the San Pedro River and grained their horses at a way
station on the other side, where they had their first word of
Bodine. He had stopped there a couple of hours earlier and
had traded their worn horses for three fresh mounts. One
of the men with him had been in pretty bad shape. Bodine
had to saddle the man's horse and even had to lift him up
in the saddle. The wounded man's name was Rawlings,
the stationmaster had said. He had no idea they were
outlaws.

Luke and Lorene also exchanged mounts, she to a
fresh stage-line horse and he to his own sorrel gelding,
which had been stolen by Bodine in El Paso and was still
in good condition after the hard ride and short rest.

"Think you can go on?" Luke asked Lorene as they
left the station. "We're not far behind them now. Tracks
show they're moving slow."

"I think I've got my second wind. I don't hurt where
I used to hurt anymore."

"It's been a long ride."

"The longest I've ever been on. But you'll need me,
Luke, if you catch up to them."

"Bodine would kill you in a minute, woman or not."

"I know. Chastity said the same thing."

Luke said nothing. Bodine was desperate now. He
had a wounded man with him and fresh horses. Tucson
was just ahead, no more than half a day's ride away. They
could expect to catch up to him at any time. As they rode
on, Luke looked hard for telltale clouds of dust, but the
valley gave up no secrets until half an hour outside of
Tucson.

The lone rider appeared small in the distance, coming
at them from the west. The horse's reins were slack, and it
plodded along aimlessly. The rider, as they drew closer,

was slumped in the saddle as if dazed or dozing. Luke slowed and pointed. Lorene saw the rider then, and opened her mouth in surprise.

"Who is it?" she asked.

"Rawlings, maybe. You hang back. If he makes any sudden moves, you duck."

"He looks hurt."

Rawlings, as if hearing their voices, straightened up. He looked around, then saw the two riders coming toward him. He weakly tried to turn his horse, but the animal kept coming east on the trail. Rawlings whimpered and sagged, almost falling from the saddle.

Luke held up his hand to halt Lorene, then reined in his horse. "Rawlings?" he asked as the rider came near.

Rawlings squinted into the sun. "You the bounty hunter?" he asked, his voice raspy.

"Luke Faraday. Where's Bodine?"

"Faraday. Yeah. Bodine and Peeker? Maybe in Tucson. I dunno. They left me." He was lightheaded. It was as if his head was floating above his body. He looked at the man facing him. A big man with a hard face—no mercy there. Well, the damned bleeding wouldn't stop. Hell, if only he could have made it to Tucson . . . but he didn't know where Tucson was anymore. Bodine and Peeker had just kept riding on, getting smaller and smaller until he lost them. Then he'd fallen off his horse and had to chase it down. The wound had broken open, and he'd taken a long time to get back up in the saddle. And then the sky and the hills began spinning and here he was, going the wrong damned way.

Luke looked at Rawlings and saw the caked dirt, the dried blood. The wet blood, too, running down his side in front—lung shot, maybe. Rawlings wheezed when he drew breath, and his eyes were dulled, rimmed with dust.

"I want Bodine," Luke said. "If you'll surrender your weapons, we'll get you into Tucson and put you in the marshal's custody."

Rawlings tried to laugh. It hurt him, and he doubled

over, straightening quickly. A wary look came into his eyes. "They'll hang me, for sure."

"You're hurt bad, man. Give it up."

Lorene rode up beside Luke, concern in her eyes.

Rawlings tried to focus on Lorene. He saw strands of coppery hair streaming from her hat—saw her breasts prominent under the shirt she wore. He looked at her face. A shadow passed across his own.

"You got a woman chasin' us? A damned woman? What the hell kind of bounty hunter are you? Ain't no woman gonna take me to justice."

"Dammit, Rawlings, don't—"

Luke knew it was too late even before he spoke. Rawlings rammed his arm down to his side, his fingers clutching for his pistol. His hand grasped the butt, and he pulled the revolver out of the holster.

Faraday's hand flew like a hawk's shadow to his own pistol. He cleared the holster before Rawlings could bring his barrel up. Sadly, Luke hammered back and squeezed the trigger in one fluid motion. The pistol bucked in his hand. Smoke bellowed out the barrel.

Lorene sighed. It all happened so fast.

Rawlings jerked as the bullet caught him in the heart. He let his pistol slide from his numb fingers, looked up at the teetering sky, and toppled from the saddle.

Faraday's eyes narrowed, his face hardening as he clamped his teeth together. "Come on, Lorene. There's only two now. Bodine and Peeker. The odds are even."

She looked at him, awestruck. Smoke curled from the barrel of his pistol. It was so quiet. The dead man lay still. His horse stood there, head drooping. Everything seemed frozen in that instant. She opened her mouth to speak, but no sound came out.

Luke rammed his pistol in its holster and rode up to her. She stared at him still, her mouth open as if struck dumb.

He slapped her cheek. Hard. Her head shook from the sudden blow. "Dammit, Lorene, don't quit on me now. Are you with me?"

She shivered in the heat, blinking her eyes. "Yes," she said softly. "I'm with you, Luke. I'll go wherever you go." And this time she truly meant it.

He looked at her a long time, trying to fathom the meaning in her shimmering green eyes. For a moment, she thought he was going to grab her and kiss her. That was what she wanted. She wanted him to hold her in his arms, stroke her hair, press her to him.

But the moment passed.

"Come on, then," he said gruffly. "Let's ride."

"Yes," she said dazedly. "Let's ride. Let's keep on riding and never stop. . . ."

He did not hear her, for his eyes were set on the horizon, looking for the dust that he knew would not yet be there. Bodine would be riding hard now, free of the wounded man. And somewhere between Tucson and Fort Yuma, Luke knew, he would go for the cache of money. All the months he trailed him had told him that much. Bodine had hidden the army payroll sometime after he'd robbed the army paymaster and before he'd come to Tucson.

Without looking back at Lorene, he spurred his mount to a gallop. All the weariness drained away. Bodine was close now—less than an hour ahead. Luke could almost smell him.

Bodine did not linger in Tucson, a scattered collection of Mexican adobe huts. The few Americans who were there owned the two or three stores and held the public offices. Apaches still raided the town frequently, and almost everyone there was armed or kept a rifle handy. Bodine stopped long enough to buy grain with money Peeker had; then they rode on.

"You wonder if Rawlings is going to catch up?" Peeker asked as they rode northwest toward Maricopa Wells.

"Nope. If he makes it to Tucson, he can likely get well. But we won't be seeing him again. Now let's ride. It's a long trail to Maricopa Wells."

"Why Maricopa?"

"Because the payroll's stashed just north of there. And if we push, catch a few hours sleep here and there, we might make it before dark tomorrow and be long gone by Friday."

"Ain't that when you were supposed to hang?"

"Yeah," Bodine grinned. "Noon Friday."

After riding for two nights and a day, Chet Morgan, with Vernon Blaine in tow, led his band of outlaws to an abandoned adobe east of Maricopa Wells late Thursday morning. From here, they could see the Pima village sprawled along the San Pedro River. The crumbling bricks and partial roof of the adobe provided shade and protection.

Blaine seemed to have shrunk even smaller. Sweating, his clothes a soggy mass on his slight frame, he appeared small in the saddle. Morgan and Arneson dragged him off his horse.

"Are you going to untie me?" he asked.

"No, Blaine. I figure we can use you when that stage pulls up to make an exchange. You just sit down in that corner over there and keep your mouth shut. I may decide to waste gunpowder and lead on you yet."

Blaine shuddered. Urine ran down his legs, staining his trousers. The men looked at him mercilessly and laughed. Wade Denton shoved Blaine toward a corner, where a rat scampered out from under a pile of broken pottery. A lizard scaled the wall, blinking down at the little man with drawn up legs and a peculiar smell.

"You hide the horses, Stokes; grain 'em and keep 'em quiet. Arneson, you climb up on that wall and keep an eye out for dust. Stage is late, and that's in our favor."

Stokes moved the horses into another room and broke out the grain. Arneson climbed up on the wall and straddled it. Wade sat down near Blaine, sniffed, then moved near a window.

Into the afternoon they waited, visibly edgy over the failure of the stage to arrive on schedule. Arneson and Denton began to grumble, eager to settle for Morgan's half of the payroll loot and be gone—before a posse or the army caught up to them. But Morgan held silent, fixing the men with a cold stare as he rolled and smoked cigarette after cigarette, into the late afternoon.

"Dust!" Arneson called a while later.

"The stage?" Morgan asked, getting to his feet.

"Nope, don't look like. Riders, though. Comin' in a mighty hurry. They ain't gonna stop at the village."

Morgan ran to the doorway and stood on tiptoe. Wade stood up and leaned out the window.

"Stokes, bring a couple of rifles," ordered Morgan.

Stokes slid rifles from saddle scabbards and carried them into the next room. The horses nickered.

"I see 'em," said Wade. "Two riders."

Morgan grabbed the two rifles and threw one up to Arneson on the wall. "If they're soldiers, shoot 'em," he said.

"Glad to."

Morgan saw them then as they rounded the twist in the road, heading for the abandoned adobe. One of them looked familiar. He heard Arneson cock his rifle.

"Don't shoot, Arnie! That's Bodine! Start waving. Stand up where he can see you."

"Hell, I'll fall off this wall!"

Morgan ran outside, brandishing his rifle. In a few minutes, Bodine and Peeker reined in, skidding their horses. Both men reached for their pistols.

"Ernie! It's me, Chet Morgan."

Bodine heard him, then gestured to Peeker. "It's my pard," he said. "Come on. Looks like the hard work's already been done."

After Bodine and Peeker dismounted and tied their horses, there was a lot of backslapping and friendly cursing. Morgan told Bodine about the prison break, and Bodine told Morgan how he'd busted loose in El Paso and fought the Indians in the pass. The others listened, admiration showing on their faces.

"We ain't got much time," said Bodine. "Looks like we got a big six-way split." His eyes swept the men in the room. Then he saw Blaine, who cowered in the corner, trembling.

"You got a rabbit, I see," Bodine said.

"We don't need him now. I'll put him to the wall." Morgan drew his pistol.

Bodine put a hand on Morgan's gun arm. "No. He may come in handy yet. I got a bounty hunter doggin' my trail. Luke Faraday. The one what brang me in at El Paso. Blaine might be useful in a trade if that *hombre* catches up."

"Blaine's got a lot to answer for," Morgan grated. "I'd like to cut him up some before I put a bullet in his gut."

"We got no time for that now. This Faraday's a bulldog. He don't let go."

"You're the boss, Ernie. What next?"

"Let's head to Maricopa Wells and dig up that payroll."

"What about the split?" asked Peeker, licking his lips.

"Even shares," said Bodine, glancing knowingly at Morgan.

"Even shares?"

"That's what I said, Peeker."

"Why, that's right fair."

"I reckoned you'd see it that way," Bodine said dryly.

"Break out them horses, Stokes, and tie Blaine on one," Morgan cut in. "We got a long way to go and little time to get there."

Stokes slapped his thigh and left the room.

Five minutes later, the troop of outlaws was heading west to Maricopa Wells.

Chapter 12

Less than two hours after Ernie Bodine and Chet Morgan led their men toward the cache of payroll money north of Maricopa Wells, Luke Faraday and Lorene Martin pulled up at the abandoned adobe near the Pima village.

Faraday dropped to the ground and began reading the signs around the adobe. The tracks told him a great deal. By looking at the amount of sand filling in the depressions, he could judge how long ago the riders had left. He entered the adobe, counting the different boot and horse tracks, while Lorene waited outside on her horse.

He took off his hat, wiped sweat from his forehead, and put it back on. From the doorway, he saw that Lorene was asleep in the saddle. Her head drooped, her arms hung slack at her sides. He walked over to her, reached up, and pulled her into his arms. He carried her like a baby inside the crumbling adobe and placed her in the shade.

"Oh," she said, "that felt nice. Can we sleep here awhile? Please? I'm so tired, Luke."

He sat down next to her and slid his hat back from his forehead. "Bodine's got help now," he said.

Lorene was instantly alert. She drew up on her elbow and stared at him. "What? You mean . . . ?"

Luke waved a hand, indicating the tracks in the soft dirt floor. "I mean someone waited here for Bodine. He

156

and Peeker rode up and they talked. Horses were hidden in that other room over there. The droppings are fresh—still steaming. Then they all rode out—west, along the stage road to Maricopa Wells. I count seven men, seven horses.''

"We can't face seven men!"

"No. I want you to wait here for the stage, Lorene. Tell Morty I'm going on to Maricopa and will keep tracking Bodine. You bring the stage along, and if you don't see me, try and send a posse or the army back from Yuma.''

"You won't do anything foolish, will you?''

He shook his head. But she didn't believe him. There was the look of a hunter in his eyes. She had seen that same look when her father had been chief of police, whenever he was getting close to solving a case. There was a fire in Luke's quiet slate eyes, and she knew he would follow Bodine to hell if need be. Her father and Luke were cut from the same cloth. There was something honest and decent about them, yet they were relentless, hard men—men who cared about justice. She hadn't realized, until now, why she had been attracted to Luke in the first place. At times he frightened her, but now that she had seen him and been with him, she realized that he was not a dangerous or cruel man.

Yesterday, when he had killed Rawlings, she had wondered how he could do such a thing. Couldn't Faraday have wounded him or talked him out of going for his gun? Now she realized that neither of these had been options. Rawlings was dying, and he knew it. He had drawn first. His intention had been to kill Luke or die in the process. And when the final moment came, Luke had not hesitated, but had shot straight and true. Not wounding the man further, but killing him. Giving Rawlings what the man had asked for—release from pain. And release from the dread of strangling to death at the end of a rope while strangers looked on at a man in the most undignified, most disgraceful moment of his life. Luke had done Rawlings a favor. Some silent communication between the two men had assured the outlaw that he would at least die like a man, not dangling hideously from a gallows rope.

She understood a lot of things now.

"Luke . . . ?"

"Yes?"

"Kiss me before you go?"

He hesitated, then leaned over and took her in his arms. He kissed her hard, and she pressed her lips against his with an answering pressure. They held the kiss for a long time.

And then he was gone—after Bodine. Alone.

The Pimas were curious about the woman in the abandoned adobe. Lorene looked at them, suddenly wishing Luke had not left her alone. Feathers jutted from black hair wrapped with cloth bands. Round dark faces peered at her. She was surrounded.

None of them made a sign or spoke to her. They just stared. One of them started to touch her horse's neck.

"That's my horse," she said.

One of the Indians laughed. The others joined in. Beyond, she could see more Indians wandering across the road from their village.

"I've got a rifle. A pistol." She remembered the rifle was in its scabbard. She patted the pistol in her waistband.

More laughter. Some of the Pimas talked to each other. She could not understand what they were saying.

She backed across the open room with its crumbling windows and half ceiling of mud and straw, stepping over pottery shards, animal bones, worn-out blankets, leather scraps.

"I can shoot pretty good," she said. "I'm not afraid of you, either."

Several of the Pimas laughed, then spoke to the others as if translating what she had said. There was more laughter.

Lorene began to anger. She stepped away from the wall and started to give them a piece of her mind, when suddenly they all started running. Puzzled, she ran toward them.

Then she saw it: the stage!

Morty Tubbs was whipping at the team, but the Pimas wanted the stage to stop. They swarmed over the road, waving their arms and shouting in two or three tongues.

Lorene saw Stuart Gorman bring up a rifle. Morty knocked it down, then swerved the team to avoid hitting a band of half-naked Indians.

"Morty! Stop! Stop!" she yelled, running from the adobe.

Morty saw her and jerked on the handbrake. The stage twisted, bounced on its thoroughbraces, and skidded to a dusty stop.

"Those Indians hurt you, Miss Martin?" asked wide-eyed Stuart. He still couldn't believe that they had not been attacked.

"Hell, no!" shouted Morty. "These are Pimas. They're just curious."

"Stuart, fetch my horse," Lorene said briskly. "I'm going with you. Mr. Tubbs, do you still have my valise?"

"Safe and sound," he said, patting the carpetbag under his seat.

"Luke headed on west to Maricopa Wells. I think Bodine met up with Chet Morgan at this adobe, and they rode that way together."

"Just Bodine and Morgan?" Morty asked her.

"No. There are seven men now."

"Seven?"

"I don't have time to explain now. We've got to hurry. Luke won't face them alone—he'll keep tracking them until we catch up or send some men to help him. But he may be in trouble even as we're standing here talking."

"Well, dagnabbit, boy, get that horse over here!" Stuart started to run, and Lorene knew that she was again among friends. As she started to smile, she saw Chastity peek out the window. They exchanged waves just as the Pimas began to beat their drums and dance. Some tried to sell blankets and pottery to those inside the coach. A Pima with black face and red lips scowled at Lorene.

Lorene wondered if the whole West was mad or if it

just seemed that way. Cornwallis was trying to shoo the Pima women away from the coach. Chastity was admiring a beaded pair of moccasins. Jenkins brooded alone in a dark corner of the stage. Stack leaned against the window, his face wan, his lips pressed tight as he masked the continuing pain.

"Miss Martin," said Morty as she finished throwing her saddle in the boot and returned the courier packet to her valise, "you'd best ride in the coach. That way you can keep an eye on *you know who*. I think it's best for young Gorman to ride up with me."

"I understand."

As she entered the coach, Cornwallis pretended to ignore her.

"Sit next to me," said Chastity. "I want to hear about your adventures with that handsome bounty hunter."

Jenkins noticed her then, as if he had just awakened from a stupor. His face wrinkled into a frown. "You'll pay," he muttered. "You'll all pay."

"Shut up, Merle," said Cornwallis. But he gave Lorene a look that told her he agreed with the slightly addled Jenkins. She was about to say something when the coach gave a lurch and they were on their way. Something struck the seat, and she saw that it was a stone. Outside the Pimas, angry that no one had bought anything, were throwing rocks at the departing stage.

Maricopa Wells was a sprawl of adobes, tipis, and small frame structures on a large plain of coarse grass and alkali soil. There were six or eight wells, each with good sweet water. The stage station was situated near two wells with a large corral, a small barn, and living quarters for the stationmen.

Bodine and Morgan led Vernon Blaine and their four accomplices off the stage road, heading north past the way station along an old Indian foot trail. Several miles beyond Maricopa, the trail forked, and Bodine took Peeker along the northeast trail while Morgan and his bunch headed northwest.

These were the same routes Bodine and Morgan had taken when they cached the army payroll in two separate locations. Their current plan was to dig up their respective halves of the loot and join forces again farther northwest at the point where the Gila and San Pedro rivers met. They trusted each other to stick to the plan because they knew they would need all their guns until they were well clear of the territory. And anyway, Bodine and Morgan never had any intention of making this a six-way split. They would find the time and place to rid themselves of all their excess baggage and end this thing the way they had begun—just the two of them together, alone.

Less than an hour after the two outlaw bands parted, Luke Faraday pulled his horse up at the fork in the trail. He dismounted and carefully examined the diverging tracks until he determined which direction Bodine's horse had taken. Then he climbed back up in the saddle and continued on his trail.

Fort Yuma Deputy Marshal Ned Hoag was bored with his assignment. By rights, the army should have pursued the escaped prisoners, Chet Morgan and his three accomplices. But they said that Morgan was no longer a soldier and that they were no longer interested in his case. They had already written off the payroll robbery money—unless, of course, it was found.

With Vernon Blaine gone, there was no one in authority at the prison, which wasn't much more than a big jail on top of a hill. But since a guard and a prisoner had been killed during the breakout, Hoag had been duty-bound to hunt the escapees and a local farmer, Ezekiel P. Stokes, who apparently had been in on the operation.

So Hoag had set out with a posse composed of two other men, and they were not the best. Rather, they were all he could afford. Even so, he was paying two dollars a day with a two-day minimum. And now, on the second day, he had finally had a break. The posse had tracked Morgan and his men to Maricopa Wells and had learned from one of the men at the way station that Morgan and his bunch had been seen passing through just before dawn, heading down the stage road to the Pima village. But they had returned only a short time ago in the company of two other *hombres* and had taken the old Indian foot trail north. And so the deputy marshal had followed the trail, come to the fork in the road, and taken the lefthand path, to the northwest. And now, early Friday evening, he at last had one of the fugitives in sight.

Zeke Stokes stood up from his squatting position in the arroyo and saw Deputy Marshal Hoag. His face flushed crimson with embarrassment. His trousers still were down around his ankles, and he hurriedly pulled them up and fumbled with the buttons.

"Okay, Stokes, take your time." Hoag stood on the edge of the arroyo looking down at Stokes.

"Dammit, Hoag, you picked a hell of a time to come sneakin' up on a man."

"Where's your bunch?"

"On ahead, I reckon. I ate some bad bacon or somep'n. This is the third time I had to drop out."

Hoag nodded at the other two men with him, and they took up positions in case Morgan was nearby.

"Where you boys headed?" Hoag asked. "Look like Morgan's making for that payroll he got stashed."

"Bodine got loose, too," Stokes answered. "He joined up with Morgan down at the Pima village."

Hoag whistled. Bodine's presence put a whole new light on the situation. He had intended arresting Stokes and sending him back with one of the possemen, but now he'd need both men. And a few more besides. Hoag considered his options. He could try to raise men at the way stations, but he knew that would be fruitless. Butterfield would raise hell in Washington, and they'd feel it all the way out here eventually.

But Hoag's decision was taken out of his hands. It seemed Wade Denton had also fallen behind, but for different reason. A loose horseshoe had forced him to stop and repair it. Now, seeing Stokes's horse tied up at the mouth of the arroyo, he rode over in all innocence.

"Stokes? Where you at?"

A look passed between Hoag and Stokes, hidden in the arroyo. Hoag put a finger to his lips and shook his head slowly.

"Stokes?"

Silence.

Wade rode closer, wary now, wondering why Stokes didn't answer. He slid his rifle from its scabbard.

Hoag went into a crouch.

"Stokes, it's me, Wade."

"Hold it, Denton," said Hoag. "Drop your rifle."

Denton froze. His gaze picked up Hoag's hat and part of a gun barrel atop the edge of the arroyo.

"No!" he yelled, swinging his rifle.

A man stepped out of the mesquite and calmly shot Denton out of the saddle. His rifle clattered on stone, and he hit the ground with a *whump*, dead.

Stokes tried to make it away. He almost got to his horse before his half-buckled pants fell, tripping him. He drew his pistol and tried to shoot Hoag, but the deputy marshal was waiting for such a move. Even as Stokes drew and cocked his pistol, he knew he wasn't going to make it. There was a puff of smoke and flame, and something hard struck him in the neck. Suddenly he was sick to his stomach, and it was hard to breathe. He could get the breath inside, but it just stayed there and started to burn as if someone had sprinkled black powder down his throat and thrown a match after it. It kept burning, and he felt everything breaking loose and busting out of his chest, with lights bouncing off the rocks and with the sky swooping down at him like a dark eagle, until the eagle's wings blotted out the sky and a big black shadow spread across the land. Finally, he saw only a pinpoint of light, which seemed to hang in front of him a long time. Then it just went out, as if it had never been there at all.

The sun was just beginning to set as Ernie Bodine topped a rise and reined in his horse.

"This country all looks alike," Will Peeker said,

riding up beside him. "Flat, dried out, alkali everywhere you look."

"Why I picked it. You bury somethin' out here, first dust storm comes along makes the spot impossible to find, less'n you know where to look. Day I buried it, the wind was blowin' so fierce it covered my tracks before they left the horse's hooves."

Bodine carefully noted the mesquite clumps and stones. The place was high, less likely than others to experience flash floods. But the high area was also nestled in a kind of natural bowl, protected by clumps of vegetation from wind and rising water. He dismounted and checked three stones. Then he began pacing off a distance between the last stone and a bush. He tamped the earth with a boot, then made an X with his heel. He walked back over to his horse and returned with one of the short shovels brought from Yuma by Stokes on Morgan's command.

"Come on, Peeker. I'll get the hole started, then you can spell me. Shouldn't take long."

He dug a shaft that angled under the large bush. Peeker took over after a while.

"Keep it wide," Bodine said.

Soon the shovel struck something. Bodine finished digging, reached down, and pulled out two sets of leather saddlebags. Both were crammed with silver and paper money.

Peeker licked his lips.

"Gawdamighty, I never saw so much money." He had only seen a small part of it, actually, but his imagination counted every bill, every coin. "We divvy up now?"

"After we put this with Morgan's. You pack one of these bags on your horse. Won't be long now."

Morgan was waiting for them at the fork of the two rivers. His horse and Arneson's sported saddlebags like those Bodine had dug up, covered with dirt and alkali dust. Beside them, Vernon Blaine was still tied to his saddle. The two men grinned at each other.

"Hey," Bodine asked, "what happened to Stokes and Denton?"

"They fell behind and never caught up." Morgan eyed each of the remaining men, then patted his saddlebag and grinned. "Anybody really care?"

"Hell, no!" Peeker smirked. "Four bags, four men. Perfect 'rithmatic!"

"Yeah," Chet agreed. "Jes' as soon as I get rid of some excess baggage." He drew his pistol and aimed it at Vernon Blaine's head. He cocked the hammer. Blaine's face drained of color, and he began to shake.

"Please God, Morgan, don't shoot me in cold blood!"

Morgan's hand began to squeeze the trigger.

"Hold it," said Bodine. "We got a rider comin'." He stood up in the stirrups and squinted in the direction from which he and Peeker had come.

"He spotted us yet?"

"No, but he's trackin'. Looks like that damned Faraday. We got troubles, boys."

"And lookee there!" Arneson called out. "Back the way we come. Dust cloud. Two, three riders. And it ain't Stokes. Maybe a posse."

Chet Morgan eased the hammer down. Blaine began to breathe normally again. His ordeal the past two days had reduced him to little more than a bundle of nerves. He no longer trusted his feelings, his emotions, his mind. He was so sure that he was going to be killed that he had given up all hope. He sagged in the saddle, a lump of flesh, no longer thirsty or hungry or mindful of his personal appearance. In his own mind he already was a dead man, and he longed for an end to this torture.

"We better move," said Morgan. "Got any ideas, Ernie?"

"We loop wide to the west, then cut south and meet the stage road at Murderer's Grave on the Gila River. Nobody'll expect us to double back toward Yuma."

"No, but we're liable to run into a lot of people, too."

"Look," Bodine continued, "we got them riders comin' on from the south, with Faraday only a couple miles to the east. And we can't go north. I can name a half-dozen tribes up there now, none of them very friendly to white faces."

"Let's ride," Chet agreed. "We get separated, meet at Murderer's Grave." He kicked his horse into motion. "Might be best to head for California anyways." He tugged the reins of Blaine's horse, and the prisoner was almost thrown from the saddle as his mount took off behind Morgan and Bodine.

Peeker pulled out next, and Arneson brought up the rear. Peeker didn't like the plan, but he had no choice. Everyone knew he was carrying part of the payroll. Any objections or strange moves on his part and he was quite sure they'd put him toes down across his saddle without blinking an eye.

Murderer's Grave was a tiny way station on the Gila River's southern bank. It lay a hard fifty miles from the fork of the Gila and San Pedro rivers northwest of Maricopa Wells—fifty miles of bleak desert, with no water along the way. The place was named after a young man who had been killed there after going berserk. The man was said to have gone crazy crossing that desert. He shot his guardian dead, and the band of emigrants they were traveling with summarily shot him without mercy and buried him there.

The outlaws rode into Murderer's Grave just before dawn on Friday. They tied up the stationmen, watered their horses, and tried to get a little sleep, taking turns on watch.

Peeker had the first watch, and it was he who saw the stagecoach rumbling in from Maricopa Wells, a fresh team churning up the sand. Morty Tubbs had driven hard through the night, taking the shorter stage road from Maricopa to Murderer's Grave. And as they headed for the tiny swing station, they had no expectation of trouble, having learned at the Maricopa station that a posse had followed Luke north in pursuit of the outlaws.

"Stage a-comin'!" Peeker called.

Bodine, Morgan, and Arneson scrambled to their feet, weapons at the ready.

Blaine blinked in the morning light, bewildered, curious that he was still alive. Arneson jerked him to his feet.

"Get the horses," Morgan told Peeker.

"Yeah," said Bodine. "Get mounted. We'll take the stage."

"Huh?" said Morgan.

"Hostages."

Mounted, the four men rushed the stage, surprising Morty Tubbs and Stuart Gorman before they had a chance to resist.

The stage stopped a hundred yards from the station, surrounded by the ruthless outlaws. Lorene woke up with a start and saw Bodine outside the window, brandishing a rifle. Quickly, she concealed her pistol under her belt, buttoning her jacket.

"Everybody out!" ordered Bodine. "We'll shoot if you come out with a weapon showing."

A sleepy, disgruntled Hiram Cornwallis got out first, his hands empty, held above his head. Merle Jenkins followed. Chastity got out and immediately saw her father sitting on a horse, his hands tied in front of him.

"Pa!" she screamed as she ran toward her father. Morgan turned to shoot her.

"Let her go," said Bodine. "Help me check these other folks out."

Stack was unable to get out. He looked pale and shaken.

"What's the matter, soldier boy? You gonna fight it out from in there?" Bodine moved toward him menacingly.

"He's wounded," Lorene said sharply. "He's unarmed and can't hurt you."

"Well now, we'll see. Peeker, take a look."

Peeker dismounted, frisked Stack, then checked the inside of the coach. He threw out rifles and pistols. "He ain't armed now," he said.

Morgan made Cornwallis and Jenkins open their coats and turn around, their hands up in the air.

"What about her?" asked Arneson, pointing at Lorene.

"She ain't got no gun belt on," said Morgan, shying away from her because she was a woman.

Cornwallis stepped away from the coach. "Look here," he said. "You don't want me. You've got these others. If you let me go, Bodine, I'll use my influence as a congressman to see that you and your friends are given a full pardon for your crimes."

Stuart Gorman's eyes narrowed, as he and Morty were inspected by Arneson. "He's lying," Gorman said. "Congressman Cornwallis doesn't have any influence in Washington—not anymore. He's being forced to resign his office. We have evidence that might even send him to jail."

"The kid's crazy," said Jenkins. "Listen to Mr. Cornwallis."

"You, too, Jenkins," Gorman added, his anger welling up in him like a force he no longer could control. "There's a federal warrant for your arrest, too."

"Mighty interesting," said Bodine. "Bunch of jailbirds offering us our freedom!" Bodine alone laughed.

Arneson kept looking at Chastity and her father, who were talking out of earshot. Chastity was holding on to his hands, and they both were weeping. Arneson turned away, embarrassed.

Bodine's attention was drawn away a moment later. There was no longer time to consider the congressman's offer. A large dust cloud was approaching from the north, signaling three or four horsemen.

"Get them people in the stage," he barked. "Riders coming. Move!"

Bodine rode toward Blaine and Chastity, as Morgan, Arneson, and Peeker began forcing Morty and the others inside the stage.

"Blaine, you and your gal get in that coach. *Pronto!*"

"Leave us alone!" pleaded Chastity.

"I'll leave you dead if you don't start runnin' toward that coach!"

"Do what he says." Blaine pulled himself up and slid

from the saddle. His daughter helped him along, Bodine riding right behind them.

"Peeker, you and I'll drive the stage. They'll leave us alone, likely, once they figger it out. Morgan, you and your man keep 'em at an honest distance."

Bodine dismounted and tied his horse to the boot of the stage. Peeker did the same. The two men climbed up in the seat, and Bodine took a last look at the approaching dust cloud.

"Who in hell's back there?" Peeker asked.

"Less I miss my guess, Luke Faraday, for one."

"Why don't we just stand 'em off?"

"Because that bunch is liable to be part of a posse. They'd hem us in and starve us out. This way we got a chance. Now grab up that shotgun and get ready to shoot if Morgan and Arneson go down."

Peeker picked up the Greener as Bodine kicked off the brake and cracked the whip. The team started to move.

Peeker looked back as the stage rumbled out onto the road. All he could think about was the money back there in the saddlebags on their horses. So near and yet so far.

Chapter 13

Luke Faraday saw the stage pull away from Murderer's Grave even as he tried to get more speed from his horse. He had joined up with Ned Hoag's posse at the fork of the rivers the evening before, and they had followed the outlaws in a wide arc to the west and south. But they had lost a lot of time tracking after dark. Rather than risk getting lost, they at last had holed up and slept.

High clouds had blocked the stars from view but had dispersed shortly before dawn, and now the sun rose above the low peaks to the east. Faraday held his hand up and reined in his horse.

"Looks like we got a kink in the rope," he said, pointing at the stage ahead as Ned Hoag pulled up beside him.

"Figger Morgan and Bodine are on that stage?" Hoag asked.

"Without a doubt. Two are on the driver's seat, with two more riding horses behind. We're facing four guns, and the hostages have to be taken into consideration."

"We can run 'em down, Faraday. Lot of time 'tween here and Yuma."

"It'll be hell. Let's take out as many as we can, first. I want Bodine."

"Morgan's mine if it comes to that."

"It will," said Luke, leading the way.

Two miles later, Luke got off a shot. He knew it was wild, but it served to swing one of the two riders around, delaying him while he sent an answering shot. The ball sang away well over Luke's head.

Lorene heard the shot and tensed.

Stack was lying on the floor moaning in pain. The bouncing coach had started him bleeding again.

Chastity had untied her father's hands. She held him in her arms, crying out of gratitude and out of fear. Blaine patted her head, unable to speak.

Cornwallis hung on to a strap, his face drawn to a mask. He glared at Stuart Gorman, who sat across from Chastity. Jenkins stared out the window with dull eyes.

"We can't just sit here and do nothing," said Lorene. She pulled out her revolver and checked the cylinders. It was fully loaded. "I'm going to try and shoot Bodine."

"You'll get us all killed," said Cornwallis.

"I think Luke Faraday's back there, trying to help us!"

"Then let *him* save us," Cornwallis replied.

"Leave her alone," said Stuart. "I'll help you, Miss Martin. I only wish I had a gun."

"I've got to get outside. Hold on to my waist."

"Maybe I should try it," Stuart offered.

Cornwallis snorted disdainfully.

"No, I'm lighter—you can boost me up. I'd have trouble boosting you."

As she tried to open the door, the stage lurched, slamming her backward into Stuart, who kept her from falling. Stack groaned as he was jostled by Gorman.

More shots sounded from behind them.

"They're getting closer!" exclaimed Chastity. "Maybe we have a chance."

"I'll just lean out the window," decided Lorene. "See if I can get a shot at Bodine up there. Just hold on to my legs, Stuart."

"Yes'm," he said, suddenly all hands.

Lorene leaned as far out the window as she could.

She could see only part of Bodine's right arm and leg.

Arneson rode up alongside and saw Lorene. "Get back in there!" he yelled.

Lorene twisted and brought the pistol up, cocking it.

Arneson raised his own pistol and aimed at Lorene. He fought his horse to keep the animal riding steady.

Lorene kept both eyes open as she squeezed the trigger. The small-caliber Colt kicked in her hand.

Arneson fired a split-second later. Then he doubled up as the woman's bullet hit him just above the belt buckle. His own bullet went wild, singing over Peeker's head.

Bodine turned and saw Arneson's horse falling back. Arneson tried to hang on, but his bloody hand let the reins slip through. He fell from his horse, bounced twice, and was still.

"What the hell?"

"Somebody inside's got a gun!" yelled Peeker.

"Kill him!"

Faraday saw Arneson fall and spurred his horse to go faster. Hoag and the others fanned out, lessening the distance.

The posse began firing at Morgan, who kicked his own horse frantically. Balls of lead tossed up spouts of dust scant yards behind him. He no longer returned fire, but tried to catch up with the coach. Out of the corner of his eye he had seen Arneson go down and knew he now was alone, with virtually no protection.

"I got him!" exclaimed Lorene as Arneson fell. "Now help me get up on top of the coach," she said to Stuart.

She opened the door again, wedging herself in the opening. Her foot touched the running board. The coach swayed and lurched as she reached up and grasped for the rail.

Stuart stepped partway outside and grabbed Lorene's legs.

"Push me up!" she gasped, holding on with one hand. The other held her pistol. "Hurry!"

Peeker saw Lorene's hand and her copper hair flying in the wind. Twisting out of his seat, he began to crawl toward her across the baggage.

Lorene looked up and saw him. Stuart, unaware, pushed Lorene hard, hoisting her up over the rail.

Luke saw Peeker atop the stage reaching for his pistol. He swung his horse to the left and saw Lorene's feet kicking as she struggled to stay on the wildly swaying coach.

Luke's horse picked up speed, caught up in the fury of the race. Faraday yelled at Peeker as he cocked his pistol, hoping to distract the man so that he wouldn't shoot Lorene. Peeker looked up, saw Luke riding alongside, and quickly turned and shouted something to Bodine, which was snatched away by the wind. Bodine looked over his shoulder, then cracked the whip. The stage team picked up speed.

Luke stood in the stirrups, steadying himself. Peeker went into a crouch as he tried to get a bead on Lorene. It was the move Luke had been waiting for, and he fired. Peeker jerked as the ball hit him in the chest. He stood swaying, still aiming his pistol straight at Lorene.

Lorene looked up and saw the black hole of the barrel inches from her face. She struggled to keep from falling off the roof as she tried to bring her pistol around to fire. Peeker's shirt was stained with fresh blood. His face contorted into a mask of hatred. Lorene couldn't move her pistol hand without lifting her elbow, and her elbow was dug in, helping her stay on. As she stared in horror, Peeker's finger moved.

Luke cocked quickly and fired again at Peeker.

The ball caught the outlaw in the throat. His finger jerked the trigger, and the ball struck inches from Lorene's head, passing into the coach and burrowing into the empty seat where Stuart had been moments before.

Peeker's body stiffened. He fell backward and tumbled over the side of the coach. He hit the ground feet first, and one leg became entangled in the rear wheel.

There was a snapping sound, but the leg held in the spokes. The stage ground to a halt.

Lorene couldn't hold on. As the stage lurched to a full stop, she was thrown to the ground, landing on her back. Air shot from her lungs. Her elbows went numb. Sparks of pain coursed up her arms. The sky spun dizzily overhead.

Bodine cursed and grabbed up the Greener shotgun. As Luke Faraday jerked his horse up short in a cloud of dust, he saw that the outlaw had the shotgun pointed down at Lorene, sprawled on the ground.

"One move, Faraday, and I blow that lady's head clean off!"

Inside the stagecoach, Hiram Cornwallis found himself staring into the barrel of a small, one-shot derringer. It was held in the palm of Merle Jenkins, who had produced it from its hiding place inside his dead wife's handbag—the one possession of hers he had kept.

"What?!" Hiram exclaimed. "What're you doing?"

Jenkins stared in disgust at the congressman. In him he saw all of his own troubles. Cornwallis had promised he would get the postmaster general to grant him the contract to handle the overland mail. He had also promised to deliver the prototype Spencer repeater rifles to Mangas, and Jenkins was not so sure this had been done. He had heard no repeating rifles during the Indian attack, and his wife had been killed by a flimsy flint-headed arrow.

"Just answer one question," Jenkins demanded. "Were the repeaters in those cases?"

"What?"

"The rifles, Hiram. Mangas never would have attacked this stage if he'd gotten those rifles. That's been bothering me all this time."

"I—I, no. Now, be reasonable, Merle. We couldn't give Spencers to a savage. But he got new rifles—Enfields—big caliber."

"You sonofabitch! I'm going to kill you, Hiram, just like you got my Anne killed!"

And as Cornwallis threw up his hands in fear, the wounded Lieutenant Stack summoned the last of his strength and leaped at the gun in Jenkins's hand.

Back outside, Ernie Bodine was carefully climbing down from the driver's seat of the stage, the shotgun still pointed at Lorene. As he came alongside the door, his eye caught sight of a scuffle inside the coach. The wounded lieutenant was struggling with the man called Jenkins. Something fell from Jenkins's hand, and suddenly it was as if all the passengers had dived to the floor of the stage.

As Bodine realized what was happening, he swung his shotgun around toward the stage door. The window was no longer empty. Facing him was the soldier, and peering over the windowsill was the snout of a derringer.

Bodine's eyes went wide, and he frantically brought the shotgun up.

Stack squeezed the trigger. Nothing happened. Quickly, he cocked it and squeezed again, just as Bodine's finger moved inside the trigger guard of the shotgun. The little derringer exploded with flame and smoke. The ball struck Bodine in the chest. He staggered backward, a look of surprise on his face. The shotgun dipped. One barrel went off, spanging the coach with dirt and shot.

Luke raised his pistol to finish Bodine off, but at that moment Chet Morgan came riding around in front of the stage team, headed straight for him. The posse, led by Hoag, was milling around on the other side, wondering what was going on.

Bodine fell down, dropping the Greener. Blood bubbled from a hole in his chest, but his eyes were clear. He drew his pistol and struggled to aim it at the nearest target—Lorene.

Morgan fired at Faraday. The ball struck the saddle, ripping a thumb-sized chunk of leather from the pommel and splintering the wood underneath. The horse reared. When it came back down, Morgan was close enough for

Luke to see the unshaven hairs on his face and the curled-back lips. Luke fired from the hip.

Morgan pitched from his saddle, clutching wildly at a bloody hole in his neck.

Lorene dove for the shotgun Bodine had dropped.

Bodine held the wavering pistol in his hand, trying to bring her into focus. She grabbed up the Greener, rolled and swung it to bear on Bodine's face. She pulled the trigger and the other barrel went off with an explosive roar. Buckshot slammed into Bodine's face, neck, and chest, driving him backward. He twitched and lifted a hand, clawing for something—something that wasn't there. He tried to speak, but his mouth filled with blood.

Lorene, shaken, backed away from him in horror.

Bodine's hand closed on something only he could see, and then it fell slowly down to his side. He shuddered as his eyes glazed over, then he was still.

Luke swung down and swooped Lorene up in his arms. "Are you all right?"

"Y-yes, I think so." She looked away from Bodine's empty, staring eyes and buried her face in Faraday's chest. The sobs came then, shaking her body as he tightened his embrace, locking her away from the brief, sudden carnage.

Morty Tubbs and Stuart Gorman climbed out of the coach. Hoag's men held pistols on them.

"That's Morty and a passenger," said Hoag dryly. "Around to the other side."

Hoag saw that Bodine and Morgan were both dead. Will Peeker, still caught in the wheel spokes, was miraculously alive. But he was dying.

"Did you get Bodine?" he asked Luke as the bounty hunter leaned over him.

"He was got."

"Good. I never did like the bastard."

"You have any last words, Peeker?"

"We got the money. More money'n I ever saw."

Luke looked at Hoag. Tubbs, Stack, and Gorman were looking on. They exchanged quick glances.

"It was never your money, Peeker," said Luke.

"For a while it was. I was rich."

Luke stood up. Hoag's men tried to get Peeker's leg out of the wheel spokes. The leg was broken in three or four places. Peeker never even felt it. He died with an idiotic grin on his face, letting out a big sigh that was the last of his breath.

Hoag walked away, took off his hat, and fanned the sweat beaded up on his face. Morty and Stuart followed him. "That all of them?" he asked Morty.

"Them, yes," said Morty confidentially. "But we got a pair more for you in the stage."

"What's that, Tubbs?"

"Them two passengers in there. One of 'em's got a federal warrant out for his arrest." He produced the papers and handed them to Hoag. "Calls hisself Jenkins, but his name's Jeffries."

"That's one. You mentioned two."

Stuart stepped forward. "The other one's Congressman Hiram Cornwallis. Miss Martin has papers that prove he'll be wanted soon in San Francisco. Can you take both of them to Yuma?"

"I don't know."

Stack came up then, having overheard part of the conversation. "The congressman also helped furnish rifles to Mangas and his bunch. They attacked us. I'll testify to that."

"You want me to arrest them now?"

Morty cackled and slapped his leg. "No, Marshal," he chided, "why don't you pin a medal on their butts and invite them to tea?"

Hoag's face clouded, but he got the point.

"I'll look at the papers Miss Martin has," he said curtly. "Meanwhile, I got a mess to clean up here."

Chastity came out of the coach now, and Stuart Gorman hurried to her side. Her hand sought his as she stood looking grimly at the bodies of Ernie Bodine and Chet Morgan.

"It's all over," Stuart reassured her.

"And it's Friday, the day they were supposed to hang," she whispered. "They tried to cheat the hangman, but didn't even make it to noon."

Fort Yuma was a scattering of buildings on the west bank of the Colorado River, near the mouth of the Gila About a mile below the fort, the adobe houses of the local settlement squatted in the sun, people milling about them They looked up at the fort and at the stagecoach outside trying to see if the people were boarding yet.

It was quite an occasion. The fort had been celebrating for a week. The story of the stage run had been carried by dispatch riders east and west along the line. Colonel George Nauman, commander of Fort Yuma, had his three companies of U.S. Artillery lined up in full dress to bid farewell to those heroes who were going on to San Francisco Troopers stood by the stage at attention. This was a special stage, departing at ten a.m. instead of three a.m., sent from San Bernardino by John Butterfield himself.

Music drifted down to the adobe settlement that some day would be officially named Yuma, but was now known as Arizona City. The ferryman sat up on his perch, listening The sound of drums and bugles carried on the air, strangely distant, broken up by the wafting breezes.

Morty Tubbs waddled up to the new stagecoach and touched the paint. The vehicle wasn't a Concord but was much like Butterfield's regular coach in appearance, except that its wheels were smaller and its top frame was covered with heavy duck. Inside, the three seats could be adjusted to form a bed where passengers could take turns sleeping. Heavy leather on the duck curtains protected the occupants from rain and cold. The interior, like the Concord's, was lined with russet leather and had cushions of the same material. Morty looked inside and grinned. The lamps were candles enclosed in wire-mesh cages—much better than the oil ones he had devised.

He waited for the others, sassy as a spring rooster.

At last the music stopped. A few moments later Lorene Martin walked over to the stage alone.

"Where's Luke?" asked Morty.

"He'll be along. He's getting our rewards."

"You mean . . . ?"

"He insisted we share it. The bounties on Bodine and Morgan were sent by draft."

"And Cornwallis?"

"The troopers are bringing him down from the prison now." Jenkins, or Jeffries, had been taken to San Francisco the day after the stage had arrived. Lorene had sent along the papers from Senator Bell to her father and had waited for the warrant on Cornwallis to come by return mail. It had arrived on Wednesday afternoon.

The stages were back on schedule, except for this special one. Mangas Sangrías and his warriors had been decimated and driven off by the cavalry. Some of the Enfield muskets had been captured and would be used as evidence against Jeffries and Cornwallis.

The others came over to the stage then.

Chastity Blaine and her father, Vernon, walked proudly, arm in arm. They did not board the stage, but stood to one side where the other dignitaries and well-wishers were forming. Morty had seen quite a change in Vernon—and in Chastity as well. The color was back in her cheeks. She smiled without that darting look of fear in her eyes. At first she had jumped at every sudden noise, like at the banquet at the fort the first night after they arrived. But after the first clatter of dishes, she had realized that her nightmare was over. Vernon had learned a sober lesson himself. Men were men and should be treated as such, no matter what their circumstances. Last night, at a formal dinner given by Colonel Nauman, he had announced that he hoped someday to run a big prison on the Colorado River—one that was tough but humane.

Stuart Gorman separated himself from a group of giggling young ladies and walked over to stand by Chastity and her father. He beamed as she reached out for his hand and squeezed it. Morty looked at them, feeling a little proud. After all, they had fallen in love on his stage,

despite the trying circumstances. Now young Gorman was
staying on in Yuma. Vernon Blaine had hired him as his
new assistant. He would not be a deputy warden, but he
could learn the business if he wished.

Stuart saw Morty, and they waved at each other.

Lieutenant Horatio Stack came over, hobbling with a
cane. He stood with the spectators also. He was going in
the other direction—back to Fort Bliss, where he was to be
decorated for valor. His bravery had been the talk of the
fort, and Morty was proud to have been a big part of that.
Luke Faraday had put in plenty of praise for the young
trooper, too.

Faraday followed Stack and stopped to say a few
words to him, slapping him on the back. The two men
shook hands, then Stack saluted Luke—and no one dressed
him down for it.

Luke was sound as a silver dollar. He was also
deputized. It was his job to take Cornwallis back to San
Francisco to face charges.

The guards from the prison rode up then, flanking
Cornwallis. His hands were cuffed. Blaine had seen to it
that he had fresh clothes. He was helped down and es-
corted to the coach. Morty opened the door as Luke came
up and took official custody of his prisoner.

"I'm ready to face my accusers," said Cornwallis
haughtily.

"Well, a week in Yuma Prison will do that to a
man," said Faraday, and Morty cackled.

"Sir, I am innocent until proven guilty."

"You can talk about that on the way to San Francisco,"
Luke replied, helping the man board the coach. "Sit
tight."

Lorene came up to Luke and touched his arm. "I'm
excited we're finally going to San Francisco," she said. "I
can't wait for you to meet my father."

"I'm looking forward to it."

"You'll stay with us, of course."

He looked at her, a slow smile spreading across his
face. "If there weren't so many people looking on, I'd

kiss you right here. I hope to stay up there a spell—if you want me to."

She blushed, and Luke thought she was the prettiest woman he'd ever seen. They had spoken a lot while enjoying the fort's hospitality. And they had stood outside looking at the desert under the soft moonlight, holding hands. They had kissed more than once, but it was never enough. Still, she seemed uncertain of him, and he supposed it was because he was not much good with words. Now he wished he could tell her how he felt.

He gently squeezed her hand. "Better get aboard," he said, "or we'll both get carted off to Blaine's hotel!"

Impulsively, she stood on tiptoe and kissed him hard on the lips. A roar rose up from the spectators, followed by a round of handclapping that rippled on the dry desert breeze.

Lorene was inside the coach then, leaving him to give a mock bow to the assembly.

"You better hop in, Luke, before you make a damn fool of yourself," Morty grinned.

Morty himself had much to be proud of, and he looked neat in his new pants, patterned shirt, and Stetson. His beard was trimmed and his teeth brushed relatively free of tobacco stain. Indeed, he had been invited to drive this special stage to San Francisco, where he would receive a cash award from the Butterfield Overland Mail Company for meritorious service.

Luke pulled the door shut and stretched out his legs. The coach seemed huge with just the three of them in it.

Lorene looked at him and smiled. He grinned back sheepishly.

They heard Morty climb up on the driver's seat. He would get a relief driver in San Bernardino, but he gloried in this moment. He doffed his hat, freed the lines, and jiggled the traces. The team stomped restlessly, anxious to move out.

"Wave, silly," said Lorene, leaning out the window, "or they'll think we're doing something else in here."

As Luke leaned out the window and waved, he wondered if his old life was finished. The Apaches were being driven out and cut to pieces. The Pima Indians were almost tame now—oddities for tourists. The Overland Mail Company was helping to change the land. John Butterfield had shortened the distance from St. Louis to San Francisco and now guaranteed delivery of the mail in twenty-five days or less. He had surveyed the route, built roads, leveled grades, built ferries and bridges, dug wells, and constructed stations. He had inspected most of the route, bought eighteen hundred horses and mules, made trial runs, planned the schedule, and made sure food and forage were available at every station. He had ordered two hundred fifty regular coaches, special mail wagons, water wagons, harness sets, and various accessories. He had spent almost a million dollars before a single coach had left St. Louis, and now more than a thousand people worked for him, including divisional superintendents, conductors, stationmasters, blacksmiths, drivers, veterinarians, wheelwrights, helpers, herders, and mechanics.

Those people had families and friends. People were streaming into the West faster than ever before. With people, the law would come in increasing force. It was stretched thin now, but it was here. And maybe the days of the bounty hunter were numbered. If, as many said, the railroads would follow the stage, then Luke's own days in the wild were numbered. Maybe San Francisco was the place to go.

Faraday waved again, wishing the stage would get rolling. The spectators waved back.

Morty yelled at the team, and at once they were off, headed for San Francisco.

Lorene pulled Luke back inside, hugged him hard, then kissed him. "You know," she said, "my father writes that he might have a place for you as a federal investigator. I was saving that bit of news for last. Interested?"

Faraday looked at the special seats that could be made up into beds. He patted them, then looked at the sullen Cornwallis sulking in the far corner. "I was just wondering when we could turn these into beds, and what we're going to do with him when we do.''

"Luke, you're impossible!''

"No,'' he said quietly. "I'm possible. And that job sounds mighty fine to me—if it means you'll be part of it.''

"What do you think?''

He was thinking a lot of things.

Coming in December 1983 . . .
STAGECOACH STATION 9:

SONORA
by
Hank Mitchum

In the summer of 1852, a stagecoach labors up a steep grade en route to the prospering gold-mining town of Sonora, California. On board is Sharon Cortland, a vivacious twenty-two-year-old blonde, journeying from her family farm in Maine to search for her brother, who had joined the rush to the gold fields but has not been heard from since. Sharing the ride is Dan Prentiss, a personable young man looking for gold himself, whose pulse races every time he looks at Sharon. Also on board are Belle Harper, an attractive middle-aged woman seeking a rich husband, and Dean Stratemeyer, a Pinkerton detective determined to end the depredations of the outlaw called the Sonora Kid.

Sharon becomes increasingly desperate as she tries to locate her brother, and Dan is discouraged when he is unable to help. Then together Sharon and Dan discover the depth of their courage and feelings when they find themselves alone in the wilderness pitted against a mysterious, demented outlaw out to destroy the stage line—and have his vengeance against those in Sonora he holds responsible for the tragic violence he suffered long ago.

Read SONORA, on sale in December 1983, wherever Bantam paperbacks are sold.

STAGECOACH STATION 8:

FORT YUMA

by Hank Mitchum

As the big Concord stage prepared to leave El Paso, the tall, lean bounty hunter Luke Faraday agrees to ride shotgun so that he can keep an eye on Ernie Bodine, an escaped outlaw he caught who is being returned to the territorial prison at Fort Yuma. But as the prisoner is being brought up from nearby Fort Bliss, his gang springs an ambush and escapes with Bodine and the empty stage.

As the army sets off on the trail of the outlaw gang, Luke and the passengers board a new coach and continue the journey. On board is Lorene Martin, a flame-haired, green-eyed beauty who is returning from Washington, D.C. with secret papers that will convict Hiram Cornwallis, a congressman and fellow passenger, who is plotting with another passenger to destroy the Butterfield stage line and set up their own. To achieve their deadly aims, they have armed a renegade band of Apaches whose desire is to rid the Southwest of all non-Indians.

When one of the passengers is kidnapped, Luke and Lorene brave attack by Indians and outlaws as they set off on a desperate mission to free the hostage and bring Bodine's gang to justice.